ITS BEGINNING TO LOOK A LOT LIKE HOMICIDE

LEIGHANN DOBBS

CHAPTER 1

The afternoon sun was low in the sky, casting long shadows across Yule Notch as I drove into town. A fresh blanket of snow had fallen overnight, covering the world in a layer of sparkling white, making the small New Hampshire town look like a Christmas postcard come to life. Someone had been up early plowing the main road. Tire tracks, crisp and clean, cut through the snow that still blanketed the rest of the landscape.

As I steered up the inn's driveway in my old pickup truck, my heart did a little jig. The old Victorian home stood tall, a welcome silhouette against the winter sky.

"This is yours now, Annie. The Yule Drop Inn," I whispered, my lips tracing the words.

Parking, I took a deep breath of crisp, cold air.

When I stepped out, the snow crunched a welcome under my boots. Afternoon light dappled the frosted pines, sprinkling a diamond-dust sparkle around me. The inn stood majestic yet hospitable, its windows twinkling hellos in the sunlight.

I pushed open the front door, and a homey vibe washed over me. This had been Aunt Ivy's realm. Flashbacks tumbled. I could almost envision her bustling around the old place, her welcoming grin infectious. Silence filled the inn now, but her essence lingered, infusing every corner. The scent of pine and cinnamon, the characteristic creaks underfoot, her mark on every bit of antiquity—the inn wasn't just a building. It was Ivy's bequest and my inheritance.

A lump formed in my throat as I toed off my boots and paced farther in. The mahogany staircase, grand fireplace, and snug corners offered plush seats. My great-aunt had been an influence on me when I was a child. I'd spent numerous holidays at the inn. Sure, I hadn't been there much since I was a teen, but her recent loss was a gut punch. This gift of the inn felt like a balm, an opportunity to hit Refresh.

My thoughts meandered to my city life—the relentless hours, the imposing caseloads, the stress that permeated my very being. I recalled my chaotic desk, the teetering piles of case files, and the perpetual duel for justice amid shrewd defense lawyers. I shook the memories away. That was yesterday.

If city life had taught me anything, it was that surfaces lied. People harbored secrets buried under layers of cordial smiles. But surely, that was a city thing. This snowy hamlet would be different, right?

A subtle noise, like the scrabble of tiny hooves on frozen ground, broke through my contemplation. My heart thudded in my chest, the sudden shift in my serene surroundings putting me on high alert. I was a city girl, and any unexplained noise got my adrenaline pumping.

I stepped out onto the back porch, the cold wooden planks a sharp contrast to the warmth of my socks. Snowflakes began to twirl from the darkening sky, landing on my cheeks with a cool kiss.

I spotted movement near the tree line—a small, huddled form struggling against a snowbank. It was a baby deer, its feeble limbs plunging in and out of the fluffy snow, a shimmer of panic visible in its wide black eyes. At least, I *thought* it was a baby deer.

"You sure don't look like the ones I've seen on TV," I muttered. I thought deer were bigger. But I was from the city. What did I know about wildlife? In Manhattan, the wildest thing I'd encountered was the occasional overly bold pigeon. Did deer attack people? I didn't think so.

Summoning my courage, I trudged through the powdery snow, my socks immediately becoming wet and my feet frozen. The deer looked impossibly small, with strange ears poking out of its head, but it had antlers, it was the right color, and it looked like it needed help. I noticed subtle indents in the snow leading to the woods. Footprints? If so, they had been snowed over by a recent storm.

"Here, little guy. Are you stuck?" I held out my hand creeping closer. Something purple and shiny was tangled in its antlers. A garland?

With a surprisingly agile leap, the tiny creature sprang over a snowbank. Startled, I gave chase, but my clumsy city legs and inappropriate footwear were no match for this nimble forest animal.

With a sudden, unexpected spin of the world, I found myself on my back, the icy crunch of the snow against my sweater a sharp contrast to the heated rush of adrenaline surging through my veins. The world swam above me, and I groaned, squeezing my eyes shut as I took mental inventory of my bones to see if anything was broken.

Suddenly, a wet, warm sensation traced my cheek. Cracking an eye open, I found myself nose to nose with the baby deer. As my gaze cleared, I noticed we were not alone. Three elderly ladies loomed over me, seemingly more interested in my predicament than in the plight of the baby deer.

With a thin cackle of dry amusement, a voice drew my attention. "Well, aren't you a sight," one of the women said, her silver hair pulled tight into a bun, spectacles magnifying the gleam of mischief in her sharp eyes. She stretched a hand toward me. "Agnes, at your service, and this here is Betty and Doris." She nodded at the other two.

"Are you Annie?" Betty asked in a much softer voice, her rosy cheeks dimpling.

Caught off guard, I nodded. "Yes, how did you know?"

The third woman, Doris, gave a soft chuckle, her face a landscape of warm wrinkles. "Ivy did love to talk about you, dear. We knew you were coming, so we figured we'd come over and welcome you to town."

"You're friends of my aunt?" I asked, already feeling warm at the thought of these ladies making a special trip to welcome me. I remembered Ivy talking about "the girls" but couldn't remember meeting them.

The three of them exchanged an ominous look

that faded some of the warmth. "Indeed, we are. Her best friends, I'd say."

I clutched the deer in my arms, its tiny nose burrowing against my neck, a flurry of warmth against the chill. My mind spun trying to keep up, taking in the friendly faces and the absurdity of my predicament.

Betty, the rosy-cheeked woman, tilted her head. "How on earth did you end up on the ground?"

"I was rescuing this baby deer. It got stuck and—"

A sudden burst of laughter cut me off. "That's no deer, dearie," Agnes managed, her words interspersed with gleeful chuckles. "That's a chihuahua!"

"Someone put reindeer ears on him!" Betty reached down and tried to remove the antlers but they seemed to be stuck. She tugged and pulled and finally, unfastened something beneath the dog's chin. I should have noticed they weren't real antlers. Betty looked them over. "Well, they are quite realistic."

The dog looked up at me with hope in his deep-brown eyes.

"Do you know who he belongs to?" I asked the three ladies.

They shook their heads. "You'd better take him in, and you can ask Nora down at the animal center tomorrow. It's right on Main Street. It's too late today. She's closed by now," Doris said.

"He can't have been out here long, he'd have frozen," Agnes said glancing over at the side of the house. "Maybe he was sheltered in there." Agnes pointed to a small little shed attached to the house. It was open and inside a blanket and bowl.

"He'd be safe and warm in there," Betty said. "And that bowl looks like food was in it. Maybe Ivy was feeding him?"

A gust of frigid wind blew by, making us all shiver. Agnes, rubbing her gloved hands together, nodded toward the inn. "For now, let's get inside. A hot choco- late sounds just right now. What do you say, ladies?" She didn't wait for an answer, already marching toward the back door of the inn.

With a last look at the tiny creature nestled in my arms, I followed the ladies inside. A new town, a new home, and a new temporary pet—my life was certainly taking an unexpected turn.

THE DOOR SHUT BEHIND US, keeping out the biting cold. I gazed around the inn's kitchen, which was untouched since Aunt Ivy's sudden departure. The cozy room held the faint scent of cinnamon and warm bread, a testament to many a joyous meal.

Agnes rolled up her sleeves and started rummaging through the cupboards for mugs. Apparently, she knew where everything was. Doris patted a sturdy oak chair, beckoning me to sit at the wide pine table in the center of the room.

"So, Annie," Agnes began, setting a kettle to boil, "what's your plan? Are you going to reopen the inn?" The clink of porcelain mugs being set on the table filled the momentary silence.

"I think I will." The words came out with more confidence than I felt. Yet in that instant, I knew it was the right decision. "It's what Aunt Ivy would've wanted."

"Good." Betty's voice held warmth, and her smile was genuine and encouraging. "She'd like that. It was her pride and joy."

Meanwhile, the Chihuahua danced around happily, occasionally pausing to sniff at various items, his tiny tail wagging excitedly. He was undeniably adorable, and my heart was already softening toward him.

Betty squinted at the dog. "Doesn't he look a bit on the thin side?"

I cast a glance at the Chihuahua. He did seem to be

all bones and big, hopeful eyes. "Maybe we can find something for him to eat around here." Cupboards creaked open one by one under my inspection until I hit the jackpot: a can of dog food.

"Well, look at that," I murmured, my surprise mirrored in the three pairs of eyes watching me. "Aunt Ivy had dog food."

A bark and a whirlwind of tail wagging confirmed the dog's approval of my discovery.

Betty chuckled. "Such an enthusiastic little guy. It's as if he's prancing."

Agnes, after rummaging through another cabinet, turned around with a triumphant grin, a tin of short-bread cookies in her hand. "That's what we should name him. Prancer."

"I..." I trailed off, looking from the dog—Prancer—to the three ladies. Naming him felt dangerously close to claiming him. The word hung in the air, an unanswered question.

Agnes just shrugged. "Well, we can't keep calling him 'the dog.'"

And so, Prancer it was. I set the bowl of food on the floor for Prancer, who wasted no time before digging in. I found another bowl and filled it with water.

The kettle whistled, and the rich aroma of cocoa began to fill the air. Agnes poured the hot cocoa into four mugs, Betty set the cookies on a plate, and we all sat around the table.

"Now, tell us about yourself. Ivy said you had an important job," Agnes said.

With a fresh mug of cocoa warming my hands, I took a deep breath. "I was a paralegal down in Boston, for a large criminal law firm."

Their eyebrows rose in unison, curiosity sparkling in their eyes. "Did you work on any interesting cases?" Doris asked, her voice slightly hushed as if we were sharing secrets.

"A few," I replied, purposefully vague. My mind flashed back to the chaos that had engulfed my life. I thought of the case files I'd been meticulously organizing, the startling discovery I'd made about my unscrupulous coworker, and the unjust accusations that had followed. But that was a chapter I didn't want to dwell on.

"Murders? Theft?" Agnes ventured, her eyes gleaming with fascination.

"Both, among other things," I said, forcing a smile, eager to change the subject. "But I'd rather hear more about Aunt Ivy. I didn't get to visit her as often as I would've liked."

The room seemed to soften at the mention of Ivy. "She loved running this inn," Betty shared, her eyes distant. "But she was slowing down. I think that's why she started closing the inn for the last week of November. She said she needed to clean it out for the Christmas rush, but I think she just needed a rest."

A pang of sadness hit me as I realized I'd missed so many years of Ivy's life. "It's just... I can't believe she fell down the stairs." My voice broke slightly at the end, images of the vibrant and energetic woman I knew clashing harshly with her tragic end.

"Fell?" Agnes looked at me, her face scrunching in puzzlement. "No, that's not possible."

Betty and Doris nodded, their faces echoing Agnes's statement. "Ivy was fit as a fiddle, always at yoga or Pilates," Doris chimed in. "Why, she could balance on one of those boards, what do you call it? Oh, a balance board! She wouldn't just... fall."

My brows knit together, and I stared at the three women. "What do you mean? The police said she lost her footing and fell. She was found at the bottom of the stairs."

"She was found there..." There was a pause before Agnes added, her voice barely above a whisper, "But she didn't fall. She was pushed. Ivy was murdered."

CHAPTER 2

$\mathcal{A}$gnes, Betty, and Doris left, leaving only the inn's chorus of creaks and Prancer's click-clacking claws as company. I eyeballed my pint-sized roommate. "Just us, huh, Prancer?" I let my hand drift over the velvet of the settee, worn from generations of people sitting. Prancer's tail whipped in affirmation, and he gave an obliging woof. Excellent. I had a canine sidekick.

Get a grip, Annie. This was an inn, not a setting of an Agatha Christie novel. Aunt Ivy hadn't been bumped off. Ridiculous. No doubt, the elderly trio got a kick from the idea, though. Agnes, Betty, and Doris probably had a book club for murder mysteries. Figured out whodunit by chapter two. The glint in their eyes when they'd quizzed me about criminal law cases was a dead giveaway. They fancied themselves golden-girl sleuths.

Yet as my fingers traced the mantel, I admired the antiques that reeked of history, and as I stood at the foot of the polished staircase—the site of Ivy's tumble —my confidence did a swan dive. This was where Ivy... had taken a spill. I took an involuntary gulp. The hairs on the back of my neck tingled. If I squinted, the staircase almost looked... sinister. *Great, now I'm seeing things. Is there such a thing as post-paralegal stress disorder?*

With a careful, measured pace, I climbed the stairs. I ran my hands over the smooth banister, looking for any signs of a struggle. I remembered a case from the firm, a man who'd fallen down the stairs. His desperate scratches on the wall had been undeniable evidence of his fall. But here there were no marks. My heart sank.

"Why would anyone want to hurt Aunt Ivy?" I voiced the question out loud, more for Prancer's benefit than my own.

I'd asked Agnes, Doris, and Betty that same question. Their answers were a kaleidoscope of motives and suspects, from Simon Knox, the local grinch who was in charge of town permits and inspections and who had argued with Ivy over some violation, to

Miranda Hightower, a local shop owner who suppos-edly had her sights set on George, Ivy's admirer. But none of those seemed to make sense. And then there was the surprise that Ivy had said she was going to show Agnes, Betty, and Doris. They'd had plans for breakfast, but when the three had come, Ivy had been at the bottom of the stairs. A mystery within a mystery.

Dragging my thoughts back to the present, I pushed open the door to Ivy's room. Her signature lavender scent lingered in the air, a faint whisper that felt like a ghostly hug.

As I ventured in, a wave of sorrow washed over me. Everything was here as if waiting for Aunt Ivy to come back. Neatly hung dresses danced in the closet, her slippers stood by the bed, and her toiletries sat out on the counter.

Prancer followed me along, sniffing at Ivy's things and whining as if he knew the owner would never come back to claim them again.

I moved over to the closet and touched her clothes —her favorite dress that she liked to wear to fancy parties, the polyester jackets she insisted were in fash-ion, and her favorite pink cardigan as comforting as an old friend.

My hand slid into its pocket, searching for the familiarity of a tissue. What I found instead was a small crumpled piece of paper. Not exactly the soft cottony comfort I was hoping for.

It wasn't a whole piece of paper, just a corner. Holding my breath, I unfolded it. My eyes scanned the ominous words "crossed the line." The sentence cut off abruptly where the paper had been ripped.

What the devil did it mean? I stared at the words, the note taking on a life of its own in my hand. The room seemed to shrink as I considered the message. What line had Ivy crossed?

Apparently, someone was angry with Aunt Ivy. Maybe Agnes, Doris, and Betty had been right about her death not being an accident.

Exhaustion clung to me like a second skin as I turned to Prancer. "It's been a long day, hasn't it?" The Chihuahua tilted his head at me, his ears perking up. He seemed to have endless energy, yet I could see the flicker of tiredness in his eyes that mirrored my own.

Room eight was tucked into a cozy corner on the second floor of the inn. It had always been my favorite, even when I was just a kid visiting Aunt Ivy for the summer.

As I pushed open the door, memories swirled around me, as comforting as a warm blanket. The room was a soft symphony of pastels, the wallpaper a delicate rose pattern interrupted by picture rails and the occasional landscape painting. The four-poster bed was dressed in a quilt of faded blues and pinks, and by the window, a cushioned reading nook looked out over the snow-covered pines.

I supposed that now that I owned the place, I should move into the owner's suite, but it still seemed too much like Aunt Ivy's. Maybe I'd just stay in room eight while I got things up and running.

My suitcase felt like it weighed a ton as I dragged it into the room, the wheels squeaking in protest on the hardwood floor. Prancer pranced alongside me, his paws clicking against the wood in a rhythmic tap dance. I found another bowl in the ensuite and filled it with water for him before we both ventured outside again. The night air was crisp, biting at my cheeks as Prancer did his business.

Back inside, I rummaged through my suitcase, changed into my pajamas, and scrubbed the travel grime off my face. I hesitated before switching off the lamp, casting a look at the bed. I'd never really had a pet before. I'd always been too busy with work, the same reason why I'd never been married or had kids even though I was in my forties now.

When I saw Prancer standing on his hind legs, paws resting on the edge of the bed, his brown eyes imploring, I couldn't resist motioning for him to jump up.

He hopped up, immediately finding a cozy spot right against my leg. His warmth seeped through the quilt, a comforting presence as I let myself relax. My heart ached a little as I stroked his soft fur, knowing that I couldn't keep him. He probably had a family somewhere that was missing him.

"Good night, Prancer," I whispered into the quiet room. His eyes were already shut, and he let out a snore. With a last glance at the crumpled note on the bedside table, I switched off the lamp and let the soothing rhythm of Prancer's snores lull me to sleep.

CHAPTER 3

A pale misty light filtered through the rose-patterned curtains, softening the edges of my bedroom. Prancer's delicate snores curled around the silence, a cozy soundtrack to the dawn. I stretched, my muscles aching from yesterday's exertions, and Prancer, sensing my movement, sprang to attention, his ears alert.

"Morning, Prancer," I mumbled, giving his head a pat. I wasn't exactly a morning person, but Prancer, it seemed, was, judging by the fact that he was all wagging tail and eager eyes. He danced around me as I plodded downstairs and over to the door to let him outside. I leaned against the doorway and watched him, uncertain if I should have just let him out on his own. I'd never had a dog before and wasn't sure what one was supposed to do.

He scampered off to do his business but was back within minutes, running in through the open door with the air of someone who was very much at home.

"I hope you're not getting too attached to me, Prancer," I told him, ruffling his ears. "You probably have a proper home."

Prancer just tilted his head and panted happily at me.

He followed me into the kitchen as I rummaged for coffee and dog food.

A sudden knock at the door sent my heart hammering. Who would visit at this hour?

I tugged the door open, Prancer at my side.

Standing there on my doorstep was a tall man with broad shoulders, his dark hair peppered with specks of gray. His arms were cradling a bakery box that sent waves of delicious smells wafting into my personal space. The surprising sight was made even more so by the fact he was the hottest guy I'd seen in a while. Especially this early in the morning.

"Annie?" His gray eyes narrowed as they took in my disheveled hair, which stuck out in several directions, and my owl-print pajamas.

"Umm... that's me."

"I'm Nick Stone. I think you met my grandmother Agnes yesterday? Sorry to barge in so early." He extended his free hand.

A blush crept onto my cheeks as I shook his hand. It was firm and warm, the rough skin hinting at years of manual labor. "Yes, I met Agnes."

"I guess I should have called ahead. I own the bakery in town, Mistle Dough, and thought you might like a taste of Yule Notch's finest pastries."

"Oh, thanks." I took the tray and opened the door wider. "Won't you come in? I was just trying to get some coffee on."

Nick came in, and Prancer bounced at his feet, sniffing curiously at the cuffs of his jeans.

"And who's this little fellow?" Nick asked, crouching down to scratch Prancer's ears.

"Prancer. I found him outside yesterday," I explained. "No idea who he belongs to. You wouldn't happen to know, would you?"

Nick shook his head. "No idea."

"Your grandmother and her friends are very interesting," I said as I led the way to the kitchen.

Nick chuckled, his eyes twinkling as he settled into one of the kitchen chairs. "'Interesting' is one way to put it. Agnes is quite the character. She, along with Doris and Betty—well, they're not your typical senior citizens. They know everything that's going on in town. It's almost a little scary."

The coffee pot burbled to life, filling the kitchen with the rich aroma of brewing coffee. I glanced over at Nick, feeling a bit embarrassed by my disheveled state.

"They seemed the type." I stirred a spoonful of sugar into my mug. "Did you know my aunt Ivy, then?"

Nick's smile softened at the mention of Ivy. "Sure did. The four of them were always together. She was full of life and vigor. It's a real shame, what happened."

The room fell into a comfortable silence as we both sipped our coffee. "Your grandmother mentioned something about someone called Simon," I began, breaking the silence. "Something about an argument with Aunt Ivy?"

Nick's jovial expression soured at the mention of Simon. He set his mug down with a thud. "Simon Knox," he muttered. "Always stirring up trouble. He's been a thorn in my side at the bakery too. He runs the permitting and inspections down at the town hall and is always finding something or other to nitpick about."

My heart sank a little at his words. "Ugh. I'll probably have to deal with him when I reopen the inn."

Nick gave a sympathetic nod. "Unfortunately, yes. You'll have to go through him for the permits."

"Any idea what Ivy and Simon argued about?" I thought about the note I'd found in Ivy's cardigan pocket. Had that ominous note been from Simon? Or knowing Aunt Ivy and her flair for drama, maybe she'd written it *to* Simon.

Pulling the tray of pastries closer, I marveled at the mouthwatering assortment. A cluster of Danish pastries—their centers filled with raspberry, blackberry, and marmalade, their flaky layers golden, adorned with a smattering of toasted almonds—filled one side of the tray. Next to the Danishes were three croissants. Their surfaces were crisp and browned to perfection. In the middle was a layer of cookies—chocolate chip, snickerdoodle, and peanut butter. And then, filling in the gaps was an assortment of muffins and doughnuts.

One particular delight caught my attention—a lemon-filled doughnut dusted with a thick layer of powdered sugar. As I bit into it, a burst of sweet-tart lemon curd exploded onto my tongue, conducting a symphony of flavors that had my taste buds dancing in delight.

"Oh my gosh, these are amazing," I said.

"Yeah, I can see that," came Nick's voice, pulling

me out of my culinary ecstasy. His lips were quirked in a smile, his tone laced with amusement. His response hung in the air, oddly out of place. Not knowing what else to do, I flashed him my best, hopefully charming smile.

With a final swig of his coffee, he stood up. "Well, I'd best get going. Lots of baking to do today."

I walked him to the door, with Prancer playfully darting around our feet. "Thanks for stopping by, Nick," I said, giving Prancer a scratch behind the ears. "I don't really know anyone in town, so it's great to start making friends. And thanks for the pastries. They're divine."

"My pleasure," he said, a smirk playing on his lips.

What was that about? I watched as he ambled down the driveway, Prancer yipping at his retreating form.

After shutting the door, I turned back toward the kitchen. I caught sight of myself in the hallway mirror. In addition to my Einstein hairdo and owl pajamas, I was now sporting a powdered-sugar mustache. So much for making a great first impression.

owntown Yule Notch was like a Christmas card come to life. It was bathed in a festive glow that was straight out of a Hallmark movie. Strings of twinkling fairy lights adorned every storefront, weaving between the lampposts and casting a soft warm glow on the snow-covered street below.

Scarlet ribbons and sprigs of holly decorated the lampposts, a sharp contrast to the clean white snow that blanketed the town.

A grand pine tree stood in the center of the square, tall and proud. Its branches were heavy with shimmering ornaments in every imaginable color, its tip crowned with a large, gleaming star. The smell of roasting chestnuts wafted from a nearby vendor, mixing with the sweet, earthy scent of pine and creating an aroma that was quintessentially Christmas.

The hum of holiday tunes drifted from unseen speakers, the familiar melody of "It's Beginning to Look a Lot Like Christmas" filling the air. People bustled about, their arms loaded with packages, their faces rosy from the cold. The sound of children's laughter echoed through the square, their snowball fights creating a lighthearted, jovial atmosphere.

The quaint shops lining the streets were alive with holiday spirit, their windows showcasing displays of meticulously handcrafted ornaments, stacks of delightfully thick woolen socks, and towers of freshly baked gingerbread.

I strolled toward the town square, the winter chill nipping at my cheeks. I pulled my coat tighter around me, my breath billowing out in front of me as I scanned the store signs for the animal rescue that Doris had said was right on Main Street.

My gaze stopped at a clever string of lights in the shape of animal paw prints. That had to be it. I headed over, my pace slowing as I noticed the windows were dark. On the door was a sign, Closed until Thursday.

Now what? I should have been disappointed, but there was a little part of me that was happy at the idea of being able to keep Prancer a few days longer. Then again, I might get more attached. How else could I find his owner?

Maybe someone had put up a sign. Surely, anyone looking for him would have posted all over town.

I inspected each lamppost and every store window, but there was no sign for a lost Chihuahua.

Maybe someone had called it in to the police.

Hmmm... that was not a bad idea. While I was there, maybe I could ask a few questions about my aunt's case.

As I headed toward the police station, I passed a bookstore—Rudolph's Reads—that specialized in mysteries. I made a mental note to stop in. I needed some reading material and loved mysteries.

I took a deep breath, pushing open the heavy door of Yule Notch's police station, the cold metal handle biting into my palm. Prancer trotted in behind me, his tiny body dwarfed by the imposing structure.

Inside, the smell of stale coffee and copier ink hung in the air. The lighting was harsh, casting sharp shadows and stripping away the quaint charm that graced the rest of the town. But the receptionist, a stout woman in a Christmas sweater, offered me a warm, welcoming smile, her snowman earrings jingling as she moved.

"Can I help you, dear?" she asked, the click-clack of her typing briefly stalling.

"Hi, yes, I was wondering if anyone reported a lost Chihuahua."

She frowned slightly, the action creasing her powdered face as she shuffled through some papers, scanning them quickly. "No reports of a lost Chihuahua, I'm afraid."

Her nameplate read Anita. She looked up at me with a soft, grandmotherly smile. "New to Yule Notch, dear?" she asked, her eyes twinkling merrily.

"Yes, I am," I said. "I'm Annie Winters, Ivy Winters's great-niece. I've inherited her inn."

Recognition dawned on Anita's face. "Oh, my, Ivy's place. That's the Yule Drop Inn, right? What a shame about your great-aunt. She was a beloved figure around here."

I nodded, a bitter taste filling my mouth. Beloved, yet someone had possibly wanted her gone. "Yes, it's such a tragic accident... but she was pretty spry for her age, you know? I have a hard time believing she took a tumble."

Anita's sympathetic smile faded into a thin line as she glanced past my shoulder. Before she could respond, the sound of a door opening diverted our attention. A tall, stern-faced woman in a sharp police uniform entered the room. Her name tag read Chief Liza Barnes.

She looked me up and down with a no-nonsense gaze. "What's this about Ivy Winters?"

"I'm her grandniece," I responded, offering my hand. She gave it a brisk shake, the sour look not leaving her face.

Anita busied herself with paperwork.

"Did I hear you questioning the circumstances of your aunt's fall?"

I felt my cheeks heat up at her stern tone. "I'm just... it's hard to imagine her being so careless, that's all."

Liza's expression remained stoic. "With all due respect, Ms. Winters, accidents happen even to the most careful people. It's my job to look at the facts, and so far, they're pointing to an unfortunate fall."

"Of course, but in my line of work, I've found sometimes the facts aren't what they seem."

A glint of suspicion sparkled in Chief Barnes's eyes. "So, Ms. Winters," she began, her words slow and measured like a snake sizing up its prey, "what line of work are you in?"

"Law," I responded, trying to sound casual. Why did it feel like I was confessing to a crime?

"Ah." She smirked. "Cupid, Donner, and Blitzen?"

I blinked. Was she listing Santa's reindeer? "Sorry, what?"

"That's our local law firm."

"Oh! No, I wasn't local. I was in Boston." I figured it would be smarter not to mention the name of the firm I used to work for. We weren't exactly getting off on the right foot, and I didn't need her finding out how I'd actually been fired. Not that it had been my fault, I'd been the scapegoat for someone else's bad decisions but that was water under the bridge now.

"Really? I thought you said you just inherited Ivy's inn."

"I did. That's what I do now. I *used* to work for a law firm. So maybe if you needed some help, I could look over the case files—"

She laughed but not like she thought it was funny.

"Sure, I just let random civilians look at the files. What do you think this is, Mayberry?"

I glanced out the window at the old-fashioned town. The Christmas square twinkled invitingly. I was half expecting Opie to stroll by or Barney Fife to come out from the one jail cell in back.

"Accidents happen," she continued. "Who'd want to kill your aunt?"

There was a rumble of thoughts. The unscratched

wall, the note in Ivy's pocket. And then there were her three friends who all suspected foul play.

"Well, she argued with some folks." I didn't want to mention the note I'd found in her pocket. Somehow, I doubted that Chief Barnes would be receptive.

"People argue every day, but they don't usually kill each other over it. Now, if someone stood to profit from her death..." Her gaze lingered on me, and a chill passed through me.

Was she calling me a suspect? But she had a point, didn't she? As I'd seen in most of the cases I'd worked, money was a strong motive, and I had inherited a valuable piece of property. But now I had to wonder— was there anyone else who might benefit financially from my aunt's death?

Barnes raised her brows. "Is there anything else we can help you with?"

I backed toward the door. "Nope, not at all. See you around." I turned and practically ran out.

CHAPTER 5

Frosty air bit my cheeks as I made my way from the station back to my car. Just down the block, past glittering window displays and holiday wreaths, was a coffee shop with a sign that flashed Jingle Bell Java. As I passed, I spotted Agnes, Betty, and Doris sitting at a table in the window.

As soon as they saw me, they proceeded to wave me in with comically exaggerated gestures. I could have used a coffee about then, so I pulled the door open.

The merry chime of bells above the door greeted me as I stepped inside, welcomed by a warm cloud of cinnamon, cocoa, and coffee.

Agnes was wearing a bright-red sweater and had a cup of coffee in front of her. Betty was hunched over a garishly green scarf she was knitting, a half-eaten turkey and cranberry sandwich on the plate beside her. Doris, on the other hand, was indulging in a plate of gingerbread waffles, the spicy aroma wafting across the room.

I pulled out a chair and ordered a latte from the waitress.

"Coming from the police station?" Betty asked, her knitting needles never stopping their rhythmic dance.

"How'd you...?" I began.

"Anita, the receptionist, is a good friend. She texted us." Agnes pointed to her phone on the table.

"Let me guess. Barnes was as warm as a snowman's heart?" Betty ventured, her tone dripping sarcasm.

My expression must have given me away because Agnes let out a snort that startled Doris. "Told Nick not to get mixed up with that one."

My eyes widened. "Barnes and Nick? They're...?"

"God no!" Agnes exclaimed. "She's his ex. I'm glad Nick dropped by your place, though."

Her pointed look made me frown. Was she trying to fix us up?

"I was hoping someone had called in a missing Chihuahua," I said as the waitress slid the steaming coffee in front of me. The foam on the top had an intricate snowflake design.

"No one has?" Doris asked. "That's weird. Did you ask Nora at the animal shelter?"

"It's closed until Thursday." I took a sip of the coffee.

"It's weird that no one has claimed that nice dog." Betty looked up from her knitting then squinted at me. "You have some foam on your lip."

I wiped it off. "While I was at the police station, Barnes acted really weird about my aunt's death."

Agnes snorted. "Tell us about it. She insists it was an accident. But it wasn't. I'd swear my life on it."

"I'm inclined to believe you," I said. "I found this piece of paper in the pocket of her cardigan last night."

I took out the paper, and they passed it around, each of them inspecting it as if it were one of the Dead Sea Scrolls.

"Recognize the writing?" I asked.

They all shook their heads.

"What does it mean?" Doris asked.

"Looks threatening," Betty said.

"Do you think it's from her killer?" Agnes was wide-eyed.

"Could be. But I think we need to figure out who would even want to kill her. Back at the firm, we would have a list of suspects based on motive. Was anyone jealous or angry with her, or would someone stand to benefit financially from her death… besides me?"

Agnes leaned back and took a long sip of her coffee. Then, with a determined glint in her eye, she began. "Well, there's Benjamin Thornton, the wannabe city slicker. He's been eyeing Ivy's inn for years. Pushier than a door-to-door salesman, I tell ya."

"Why would he want the Yule Drop Inn so badly?" I asked.

Agnes chuckled, her eyes dancing. "Benjamin's a developer. More interested in dollar signs than tradition. He's been bothering Ivy for years, but she wouldn't have sold to him if he were the last man on earth."

Betty picked up the thread. "Then we have Cecelia Rothschild. You'd think with her money she'd have better things to do, but no. She's always sticking her nose where it doesn't belong. Had a row with Ivy when they cohosted the Elf Extravaganza charity event a few weeks ago. After that, their relationship went sour."

"What was their argument about?" I asked.

Betty shrugged. "Ivy wouldn't say."

Agnes smirked as she leaned back. "Don't forget about Miranda Hightower. The woman could flirt with a stone wall. She was always batting her eyelashes at Ivy's George."

"Were Ivy and George serious?" I remembered Ivy mentioning him in passing but not as if he was anything special.

Doris laughed. "George was pretty serious. I don't think they ever hooked up, though."

Ewww. I wrinkled my nose at the thought of Aunt Ivy *hooking up*.

"Anyway, Miranda wanted George all to herself, but he had eyes for Ivy." Betty kept her eyes on her knitting as she spoke. "It was like a lovers' triangle."

"That's a good motive for a murder of passion, like pushing someone down the stairs. With Ivy out of the way, Miranda could have George all to herself." Agnes's eyes were twinkling a little too brightly at the idea, if you asked me.

"Let's not forget Eliot Burke, the city lawyer turned wannabe countryman. He owns the property next to the inn, and he and Ivy butted heads over property lines more than once," Doris added.

I glanced at the note again. "Cross the line... I thought it meant figuratively, but maybe if the note is from Eliot, he meant literally."

"Could be," Doris said.

"Last but not least," Agnes continued, "Simon Knox. That man can sour milk with his scowl. He and

Ivy had a big argument a couple of weeks ago. He threatened to shut her down for good."

"Why would he want to do that?"

"Who knows. He's just mean," Betty quipped. "He'll get his comeuppance in due time."

"This is all very interesting." I sipped my latte and leaned back in my chair.

"So..." Agnes leaned forward, her eyes twinkling with mischief. "Are you going to take the case?"

"Take the case? I'm not a detective or anything."

Doris locked me in a stare that was part eagle, part lawyer. "But you've got experience, dear. That much is clear."

"A smidgen," I corrected. Actually, I had more than a smidgen. I'd been studying cases for years as part of my job and directing witness statements and motivations, not to mention that I gobbled up mystery novels like they were a turkey dinner on Thanksgiving.

The three ladies stared at me with hopeful expressions.

"Look, I'm not promising anything," I said. "But... I suppose there's no harm in just... looking into these people. You know, unofficially."

Agnes beamed like she'd just unwrapped the best Christmas gift. "There's my girl! Now, you just let old Agnes worry about the bill for your latte here."

"That's very nice of you. Thanks," I said, rising from the chair. "I guess I'll head home and get started."

"Let us know right away if you figure out who the killer is!" the three of them shouted after me as I opened the door and stepped onto the sidewalk.

CHAPTER 6

That night, I sat in the kitchen of the Yule Drop Inn, making a list of what I needed to do in order to open the inn back up. Aunt Ivy had always said the holiday season was her busiest, and I had bills to pay.

Luckily, the inn was pretty well stocked and had been running in tip-top shape recently. Ivy usually closed down just for a week to get everything organized for the big rush, so I wasn't too worried about needing to get supplies. Still, I did want to get familiar with what I had.

The commercial fridge was full, but it had been two weeks since Aunt Ivy died, and many things had gone bad. I made a list of what I needed to resupply.

Surveying the hodgepodge of copper pots and

pans suspended above the stove, their polished surfaces glowing in the kitchen light, I let out a sigh. The baking basics were there—the flour, the sugar, and the sprinkling of nutmeg that Ivy had used to add a festive flair to her dishes. I was no Julia Child, but at least I wouldn't be eating takeout every night.

As I considered my culinary future, Prancer sauntered in. The Chihuahua peered up at me, his beady eyes seeming to ask, "Do you even know how to use those?"

Before I could respond to his judgmental glance, a scratching sound from the cabinets caught our attention. Prancer's ears perked up, and he ran over to it and pawed at the door.

Out of the corner of my eye, I saw something speed out from the other end of the cabinets and run under the door.

Yikes. Mice?

I opened the door, but nothing was there. They could squeeze into tiny places. Maybe he'd found an opening in the doorframe or had gotten outside. Hopefully, he'd stay out if he had.

I peered cautiously into the cabinets but didn't see anything, my heart pounding a little too fast for comfort. *Better call an exterminator.*

Prancer trotted over to his food bowl, his tail wagging. I guessed he wasn't too concerned.

I gave another glance at the cabinet, but no more sounds came. I decided I'd better continue with my inventory.

What about linens? On my inspection the night before, I'd noticed that all the rooms were made up and waiting for guests, but there would have to be extra linens for when guests checked out.

I went up to the storeroom, which was really an old servants' room on the third floor. Ivy had outfitted it with shelves and storage cupboards. Gazillions of neatly folded towels and sheets lounged on wooden shelves, ready for service. It was a sight that could make a Bed Bath & Beyond salesperson green with envy. It looked like I was set for linens and towels.

The dining room was all set with chafing dishes, glassware, and plates.

The parlor was perfectly arranged with conversation areas.

And then there were the books. Ivy's romance novels were crammed into every nook and cranny of the inn. Bookshelves were a part of every room and hallway.

Me? I was a mystery aficionado, craving the adrenaline of a thrilling chase, the mental acrobatics, and the deliciously unpredictable plot twists that could turn your world upside down. I could have used a good mystery to escape into right then, as a matter of fact.

Which reminded me of the bookstore I'd seen downtown. Maybe I'd pop in later in the day and pick out a few books.

I stood in the large main room and looked around. I did need to give the place some holiday cheer. A Christmas tree, some garlands, and mistletoe were in order. Luckily, I knew that Aunt Ivy had boxes of holiday decorations up in the attic, and I'd seen a tree lot in town where I could get a giant tree just like Ivy always had for the holidays.

Simon Knox was a thorn in my list, though. With the inn ownership changing, I'd probably need some new permits, and if what I'd heard about him was true, he'd probably give me a hard time. But a visit to him might be beneficial in other ways. He'd argued with Ivy, and I wanted to know why. Of course, he wouldn't outright tell me, but I'd seen enough lawyer theatrics back in Boston to know how to subtly pry for information.

As I mused, Prancer pranced around me, his tail wagging like a metronome. "Looks like you're staying for another day or two, buddy," I told him, scratching behind his ears. Prancer's face split into a doggy grin, and I couldn't help but mirror it.

"Don't get too attached, though. I'm sure you have a family out there somewhere," I said more solemnly. I wasn't sure if the words were meant for him or for me.

CHAPTER 7

*B*undled up against the crisp winter air, I ventured toward the town center, the wind nipping at my cheeks. The sight of Rudolph's Reads peeking between the snow-dusted shops brought a flutter of anticipation.

As I stepped inside, I was greeted by the papery scent of well-loved books and the sound of a crackling fire. A regal Maine coon lazily glanced my way from his royal throne—a plush cushion near the warmth of the fireplace.

A woman about my age looked up from her novel as the bell above the door chimed. Her friendly smile eased the winter chill from my bones. "Welcome to Rudolph's Reads." She stood to extend a hand. "I'm Maggie Sullivan."

I liked her right away. She was the kind of woman who exuded warmth and comfort. She was petite, her figure dwarfed by the towering bookshelves, but she moved with an easy confidence that filled the room. Her hair, the color of warm chestnuts, was twisted up in a messy bun. Peeking out from under the tousled strands were small silver hoop earrings that glinted in the soft light of the bookstore.

Her face, though youthful, was marked by laugh lines and crow's feet—telltale signs of a life well lived. Sparkling, intelligent green eyes looked out from behind a pair of thick-rimmed tortoise shell glasses that perpetually seemed to slide down her nose. The spectacles only added to her charm, making her seem both endearing and scholarly at once.

She was dressed comfortably in a chunky cable-knit sweater the color of autumn leaves, worn jeans, and a pair of well-loved boots. There was something soothingly familiar about her, like an old, favorite book you couldn't help but return to.

"Annie," I replied, returning her handshake. "I've recently moved into the Yule Drop Inn."

Recognition flickered in her eyes. "Oh, you're Ivy's great-niece, then. We all miss her dearly. What a horrible accident."

My brow furrowed at the way her voice dipped when she said the word *accident.* "You sound like you're not sure about the accident part."

Maggie cast a furtive glance around the store, her eyes flicking to the door and back. She leaned in closer. I mirrored her, instinctively tilting my head as she spoke in a low voice. "I'm not usually one for conspiracy theories, but, well... I am Doris's granddaughter."

"You are?" Was everyone in this town related?

She nodded. "She told me that they spoke to you about their theory and you were on board."

"Well, I don't know." Suddenly, it felt silly to be questioning the circumstances of my aunt's death. I mean, the police had investigated and determined it was an accident. But then I remembered the awful attitude of Chief Barnes and realized I did kind of want to prove her wrong.

"Ivy was just too spry to fall down her own stairs," Maggie said. "And it's not just because I spend my day reading mysteries, either. Something is not right."

"I agree, but I'm not sure how to go about proving it." I petted the cat who had jumped up on the counter.

"That's Hemingway." Maggie introduced us, and

the cat looked at me with disdain before turning his backend toward me, flicking his tail, and jumping back down.

"He seems friendly." I hoped I didn't sound too sarcastic.

Maggie laughed. "At least he didn't scratch you."

Seeing Hemingway curl up by the fireplace reminded me of Prancer. "You wouldn't happen to know of anyone that lost a Chihuahua?"

"No. Grannie told me you found one, but I have no idea." She looked at me thoughtfully. "So, who do you think would have wanted your aunt dead?"

"Good question. I have to admit that I don't really know much about her personal life. Doris, Agnes, and Betty had some ideas. What about you? Do you have any?"

"Well," Maggie began, absently thumbing through a paperback. "Gram said she favors Benjamin Thornton. He's a real piece of work—very pushy. Was always bugging Ivy to buy the inn."

"I don't know. He sounds annoying, but to kill her for the inn? How would he even know that he could buy it after that? Surely, he can't go around bumping off everyone whose property he is interested in."

"I don't know. I think I read about someone who

did that in a mystery series." She turned to survey the shelves as if looking for the series.

"Your grandmother mentioned a few others. Someone my aunt had a falling-out with over some charity event," I said, hoping to keep her on track.

"Cecelia Rothschild." Maggie turned back to me, her face scrunching in distaste. "Oh, she likes to act all important with her designer bags and fancy cars. But I heard from a reliable source she's in quite a bit of financial trouble."

"Do you know what the falling-out was between her and my aunt?"

"No idea, but now that Ivy is gone, that's going to put a big hole in our charity committee. Your aunt was such a force on there and raised a lot of money for the town." Maggie looked at me expectantly.

I supposed I could try to take over some of her charity duties. Ivy always said it was good for the inn to be involved, but right now, I was more interested in talking about suspects.

"What about the person who wanted Ivy's boyfriend?" The thought of that still made me feel weird.

"Miranda Hightower," Maggie said, a grimace twisting her features. "Owner of Baubles and Boughs down the street. She had her claws out for George McKinley. Poor guy. He only had eyes for Ivy, though."

I made a mental note to visit Baubles and Boughs.

"Then there's Eliot," Maggie continued. "Mysterious past, land disputes with Ivy. Now, I'm not one to judge, but he's been known to throw a tantrum or two over property lines."

"Aunt Ivy never told me about that."

"Lastly, Simon Knox," Maggie said, her face hardening. "The town's very own grinch. He's a pain for every business owner in town. He's even given me a hard time. Tried to say I had too many books in here and the load was too much for the building! I had to point out that one can never have too many books."

"Ughh. I have to go see him to make sure I don't need any new permits or anything with the inn changing hands. But at least I have a valid reason to try to ask some questions about my aunt. I'm not sure how I could talk to most of the others, though."

Maggie leaned in, her eyes sparkling with excitement. "I do. We have a book-club meeting tonight. Eliot and Cecelia usually attend. You should come. It's a good chance to observe them. Plus, we're discussing the mystery novel *Telling Lies* by L. A. Dobbs. Might be up your alley."

She slid a copy of the book across the counter to

me. It was an intriguing cover, and best of all, it had a dog on it. "I'll take it."

I picked out several more novels and paid for them. As I turned to leave, I glanced back at Hemingway. He met my gaze with his striking green eyes, his tail flicking with what I chose to interpret as approval.

CHAPTER 8

I put my books in the truck and drove to the town hall. It was an imposing Colonial Revival building. Its grand entrance boasted a massive arched door beneath a pair of stately columns. Though the white paint was chipping in places, a testament to the harsh New Hampshire winters, the structure stood with an air of sturdy defiance, its stone facade weathered yet undeterred.

Like the rest of Yule Notch, the inside of the town hall was decorated for the holiday season. Garlands, holly, mistletoe, and twinkling strings of lights filled the room, draping the space in festive charm.

A majestic Christmas tree was the focal point of the lobby. It towered at nearly two stories tall. The fragrance of fresh pine wafted from its lush green needles. Multicolored ornaments, each a unique shape and size, glittered in the hall's soft lighting. Tinsel sparkled from the ends of each branch. The tree's colorful lights were reflected in the polished marble floor. A tree skirt, plush and red, sat at the base.

Copper plaques were posted on the walls, with directions to each office. I scanned the list. Permitting, second floor, office 2B.

Getting to the permitting office was no easy feat. Corridors decked out in Christmas wreaths led me on a labyrinthine journey. After one wrong turn, I was face-to-face with a broom cupboard—not my intended destination. Blushing, I retraced my steps.

Eventually, a flight of stairs, glowing under the light of red and green LEDs, took me to my goal. The permitting office was tucked away upstairs, its entrance marked by a garland of frosted pinecones.

There, amid the ocean of desks and paperwork, was an office with a brass plaque to the right of the door—Simon Knox.

I peeked in to see a small man whose bald spot caught the fluorescent lighting. A frown was etched onto his face.

"Mr. Knox," I said, tapping on the door. "I'm Annie

Winters. I inherited the Yule Drop Inn. I think I might need to discuss some permit applications."

He peered at me over his thick-rimmed glasses. "Change of owner. You'll need a food-service permit, fire safety certification, and a public-assembly permit to start with. And those will need renewing annually."

I blinked, taken aback. "And why, pray tell, would I need a public-assembly permit?"

His lips curled into a wry smile. "Unless you plan on running the inn solo with no guests, you're considered a place of public assembly."

"Oh. Right." I sized him up. He was a small man, but could he have pushed Ivy down the stairs? I supposed if he were angry enough. Especially if he pushed her from behind and she didn't see it coming. She would have been taken by surprise, with not enough time to even scratch at the walls or railing to try to save herself.

He turned back to his work as if dismissing me.

"I heard you had some issues with the inn. Could you tell me what those were? I want to make sure they are all cleared up before I reopen."

For a moment, he seemed surprised, then his gaze turned cold. "Ivy had several violations. Health code, fire code, you name it."

I remembered Ivy mentioning a petty fire-code

violation last year. But she'd taken care of that. "She took care of those."

Simon looked smug. "Not the most recent one. The health violation."

"What was that one specifically?"

He leaned back in his chair, folding his arms over his chest. "Contaminants in the kitchen."

I made a face, thinking about the things I'd eaten in the kitchen. "What kind of contaminants?"

"The four-legged kind."

The mice. Crap. I moved *getting an exterminator* up on my mental to-do list. "That will be taken care of before we reopen."

"It had better be, or you won't be reopening."

I nodded, trying to keep my irritation in check. "Do you know where I can find the charity committee?"

He pointed toward a woman at the far end of the room. "Talk to Geraldine. She handles that."

Geraldine was a sprightly woman in her late sixties, her silver hair pulled into a bun so tight it looked like it could double as a face-lift device. But her eyes sparkled with kindness, and her smile was genuine.

"We had to cancel some of the charity events," she admitted, a touch of sorrow in her voice. "Money's been tight, and with Ivy gone, we're short-staffed. We're redoing the list, but if you stop by tomorrow, I might have one for you."

As I left the town hall, my mind buzzed with questions about permit troubles, charity event cancellations, and a town grinch who seemed to have a vendetta against my inn.

I CALLED the exterminator right after I left the town hall. Thankfully, he could come first thing in the morning, so I headed over to Baubles and Boughs to size up Miranda Hightower.

As I swung open the door to Baubles and Boughs, the silver bell atop jingled a tune of welcome, a sound merrily echoing through the glimmering spectacle within. Immediately, a warm current of air embraced me, scented with rich mahogany and a tempting dash of bergamot, reminiscent of an expensive perfume.

Inside, the shop could only be described as dazzling. Delicate lights were sprinkled over glass cabinets, casting their glow over an array of jewelry, making every single piece wink like a star.

Near the window was a white Christmas tree

strung with strands of faux pearls and twinkling rhinestones.

In the middle of this glamorous chaos was a woman who could only be the shop's owner, Miranda Hightower. She was every bit as sparkly and flamboyant as her shop.

Her hair, a snow-white beehive, was dotted with sparkling snowflake-shaped barrettes. She was in a scarlet dress, sequins sewn throughout. The hem dripped with a red-and-silver trim that resembled a garland. Her snowflake brooch and titanic ruby-colored earrings completed her over-the-top holiday look.

"Welcome to Baubles and Boughs!" she trilled, her smile a gleaming curve on her immaculately made-up face. It was only when I revealed my identity and my connection to Ivy that her festive cheer waned, replaced with a frosty politeness.

"Ivy's great-niece," she murmured, not bothering to hide her surprise. "I see you are just as plain as your late aunt."

I glanced down at my outfit—jeans and a black puffer jacket. I didn't usually wear jewelry and had my long hair in a ponytail. Plain? I preferred to think of myself as practical.

"Well, I can see why you came here. You need

jazzing up." Her lips stretched into a chilly smile, her gaze raking over me with the precision of a hawk. "Let's get you out of that coat so we can try on something with a little... dazzle," she said, almost forcibly guiding me toward a display of necklaces that rivaled Las Vegas for their neon audacity.

I went along, figuring it was a perfect way to get her talking. Maybe she'd let something slip.

"Were you close with my aunt Ivy?"

"Hmmm. I don't know if I would use the word *close*." She avoided the question, instead thrusting a sapphire necklace against my chest. "This would go stunningly with your blue eyes."

"Surely, Aunt Ivy would have bought jewelry from you," I said as she chose another garish necklace in fuchsia and gold.

She held the necklace up to me and tilted her head this way and that. "She didn't have a taste for finer jewelry like mine."

"But maybe George bought something for her here."

Miranda's festive facade wavered, and she snatched the necklace away. "Is that what Ivy told you?"

"No, I just assumed..."

"Well, he didn't. George is my boyfriend, not Ivy's."

Especially since she's dead now, I thought.

"Your aunt Ivy... well, she may have entertained certain... fantasies." Miranda's crimson nails glided over another piece of jewelry. "But she didn't seem to see..." Her gaze was far away, her mouth set in a tight line. "That George... George has always been mine."

I raised an eyebrow at her possessiveness. "I heard they were close."

"People talk," she said, her tone frosty. "Gossip is a small town's pastime, dear."

"True, but why would people make that up?"

Miranda huffed, a dismissive sound. "People like to stir trouble, and your aunt was always quite... dramatic."

"But—" I started to interject, but she overrode me, an icy smile fixed on her face.

"Now, how about we look at some earrings?" She picked up a pair of flashy chandelier earrings, their shiny beads glittering in the shop's light. "You wouldn't want to appear underdressed at the town's holiday festivities, would you?"

Her quick change of subject was almost comical. Almost. But a sobering thought nestled into my mind. Could Miranda's obsession with George have pushed her to eliminate my aunt? The question, unsettling as it was, left a chill in me that had nothing to do with the cold weather outside.

I managed to get out of Baubles and Boughs with only a purchase of their most modest earrings that I was sure I would never wear.

As I turned from the door, I saw Chief Barnes on the other side of the street. Was she watching me? I was probably being overly paranoid. I gave a little wave and headed toward the pet store to get some more dog food and see if they knew anything about Prancer.

AFTER I PICKED up some items for Prancer, I ventured to one of Aunt Ivy's favorite spots—a secluded bench overlooking the skating pond. Sunlight danced across the ice, which looked like a well-buttered pie crust. Skaters in colorful outfits whirled by, some with the grace of professional dancers. The scene was picturesque but missing its main ingredient: Ivy's laughter, the kind that made you laugh just at the sound of it.

As I approached, I noticed George sitting on the bench, his eyes fixed on the pond. A wave of sadness washed over me. They must have spent countless hours here together. I'd only met George briefly before and had given him my condolences at her funeral. His fondness for my aunt had been obvious.

"George?" I called out, pulling my scarf tighter. He looked up, startled.

"Oh, Annie," he said, his voice thick with emotion. "I didn't hear you coming."

I settled beside him on the bench, offering a sympathetic smile. "This place means a lot to you, doesn't it?"

He nodded, brushing a tear from his eye. "I miss Ivy so much."

I reached over and gave his hand a reassuring squeeze. That was when he noticed the bright bag from Baubles and Boughs in my grasp.

"Be careful about that woman," he warned, nodding at the bag.

"Miranda? Why? I thought you two were an item," I said, eyebrows raised.

George made a face. "Where did you hear that?"

"From Miranda," I replied, trying not to laugh at his aghast expression.

A bitter sound escaped his lips. "That figures. The woman is disturbed. She was jealous that I cared for Ivy and not her." George sighed, his voice tinged with regret. "Though Ivy didn't return my affections to the level I wanted."

His eyes narrowed, and I couldn't help but wonder if his affections had ever boiled over into anger. Was he upset that Ivy didn't love him back or just upset at her method of rejecting his overtures?

"Anyway, Miranda's the kind that would boil a rabbit, if you catch my drift," he added, giving me a knowing look.

"Do you think Miranda would harm Ivy?"

George looked startled. "Harm her? How? You don't mean... I thought she fell by accident."

His voice wavered, and a cold chill ran down my spine. Was he genuinely disturbed by the thought of someone pushing Ivy, or was his dismay more because we might find out who really did push her?

"I heard Ivy argued with Cecelia Rothschild. Do you know what that was about?" I asked.

He sighed, his gaze drifting to the pond once more. "I'm not sure. Something to do with the Elf Extravaganza charity event. Ivy was very mad about something, but I don't know what it was."

"Thank you, George," I said, standing to leave the man to his memories. "If you need anything, please let me know. I know Ivy was very fond of you."

George smiled a sad smile. "It was good to see you again, Annie."

As I walked away, my mind buzzed with new information. Unfortunately, now I had more questions than answers.

CHAPTER 9

I arrived home armed with goodies for Prancer. Food, dog toys, and a leash—even though he didn't really need one since he always seemed to run right back in when I let him out to do his business.

He danced around me, wagging his tail, as soon as I got in the door. I put the packages on the counter and picked him up. "Don't you go thinking this is the new normal, buddy. The rescue center will be open tomorrow. Your owners must be missing you something fierce."

As Prancer checked out his new toys, a sense of reality began to dawn on me. With the local rescue center reopening the next day, my reign as the temporary dog mother was short-lived. The pang of melancholy that settled in my chest was quickly displaced by a sense of dread when I looked at the stack of forms I'd gotten from Simon.

And that reminded me of the mice. Aunt Ivy had never mentioned any mice, but she probably wouldn't have. Was that one of the reasons she'd decided to close for a few weeks? The exterminator was coming in the morning, but I decided to check the kitchen cabinets more thoroughly to see what I was up against.

"All right, you whiskered squatters, let's see what you've got," I muttered, bracing for the worst. The kitchen was quiet except for the sound of Prancer's claws on the wood floor as I opened the bottom cabinet, which he'd been pawing at before.

I poked my head in.

Prancer poked his head in beside mine.

My eyes darted from one shelf to another. I half expected a furry rodent to leap out at me, but there was nothing. I poked around boxes of cereal and pasta, moving them to one side and then the other. I studied every inch of those cabinets and was thankful when I didn't see any creatures. No nests. No chewed boxes. Not even a tiny telltale dropping or a paw print in the dust.

I pulled my head out of the cabinet. Prancer pulled

his head out too. I looked at him. "That's good news. Maybe that guy we saw was just a loner."

Prancer cocked his head. He looked a little disappointed. Maybe he'd been hoping for mice.

But the thought of paw prints reminded me of something. My mind flitted back to the afternoon I'd found Prancer. I'd noticed prints—human ones—around the same area. The snowy impressions were faded and indistinct, probably two weeks old, from around the same time Aunt Ivy had taken her fatal tumble down the stairs. A shiver that had nothing to do with the winter chill stole over me.

I donned my boots and puffer jacket, casting a glance at the outdoors through the frosted window. The world was swathed in white, except for the path I'd trudged through the snow earlier and Prancer's tiny paw prints from his various trips outside to do his business. Despite the daylight waning, I felt an irresistible pull to investigate further.

I headed outside, Prancer prancing beside me, his little body almost swallowed by the powdery snow. The old footprints were there, faded but still discernible. They meandered away from my house and into the woods, where a thin thread of smoke danced from a hidden chimney.

Eliot Burke. The adjoining property owner and

possibly the owner of the footprints. My eyebrows knitted. Doris had mentioned an argument between him and Ivy about property lines. *But that doesn't mean... he wouldn't... would he?*

I stared into the distance, lost in thought. Prancer sat beside me, matching my contemplative mood. A niggling feeling gnawed at me, my mind spinning.

Why would Eliot trudge through snowy woods to the back of my aunt's place when he could have just driven down the road? The only reason I could think of was he didn't want anyone to know he was here.

"Well, Prancer," I murmured, scratching behind his ears. "Looks like we'll need to play detective tonight. Lucky for us, Eliot's a member of the book club, and the meeting is in just a few hours."

CHAPTER 10

I didn't want to show up at the book club empty-handed, especially being the newcomer and all, so I decided to bring a treat, and I knew just where to get it. Mistle Dough Bakery.

The pastries Nick had brought were out of this world and would be perfect for a book-club snack. It had nothing to do with seeing the charming baker again.

Mistle Dough was a Christmas wonderland. The gleaming glass pastry cases housed a parade of frosted Christmas cookies in the shape of Santas, reindeer, snowflakes, and Christmas trees. Perfectly rolled yule logs and enticing thumbprint cookies sat alongside every holiday confection you could imagine. The air was laced with the comforting hum of holiday tunes, and the smell of baking dough, vanilla, and warm spices hung in the air, making my mouth water.

Like everyplace else in Yule Notch, there was a large Christmas tree in the corner. This one sported popcorn garlands and gingerbread-man ornaments.

Nick came out from the back. He looked pretty good in an apron, especially with those muscles flexing and moving beneath his T-shirt as he carried a large tray of cupcakes. The frosting stains on the apron added an adorable touch to his rugged charm. I surreptitiously touched my lips, remembering the powdered-sugar mustache I'd sported the last time we met.

His eyes flicked up to meet mine, initially glossing over before lighting up with recognition. "Annie?" He looked me up and down. "Glad to see you got out of your pajamas."

Heat suffused my cheeks, but I hoped my blush was convincingly attributable to the warm bakery. The last time we'd met, my hair resembled a bird's nest, and I'd been sporting a fashion-forward pajama ensemble. This time, my dark hair was actually tamed, lying flat and shiny, while a modest coating of mascara made my eyes pop. All for the book club. Of course, it had nothing to do with the fact that I'd be popping into the bakery and might see Nick.

"Hey, Nick," I said, hoping the nonchalance in my voice didn't betray the sudden fluttering in my stomach. "I need some pastries for the book club meeting tonight."

"Ah, the book club!" Nick's eyes lit up with recognition. "My gram's a regular. I can be your pastry guide."

The shop was quiet, with no other customers. Alone with Nick, I found the scent of fresh dough and sugar a touch sweeter.

He recommended an army of cookies, pointing them out from his side of the pastry case. There were pinwheel cookies, their spirals a dazzling swirl of red and green. Chocolate chips were next, golden discs studded with semisweet morsels. Brownies were topped with almost an inch of chocolate frosting. And then came the gingerbread men, their cinnamon-scented bodies adorned with sugary buttons and royal icing smiles. I tried not to drool as I made my choices.

Our conversation wasn't just about pastries. The banter was light, and I might have thrown in a little flirty zinger or two. I couldn't help myself. The twinkling Christmas decorations, sugar-laden air, and warmth radiating from Nick's grin all felt like something out of a Hallmark movie.

"So, how's the inn project coming along?" he

asked, brushing a hand through his hair, leaving a cute dusting of flour.

"Well, I met with Simon..." I started.

At the mention of Simon's name, Nick's jovial expression soured. "Simon was here earlier, stirring up trouble. Said the electrical needed upgrading. It's always something with that guy."

"Tell me about it. He gave me a stack of forms to fill out for permits and didn't seem at all happy that I was reopening the inn."

"Don't let him discourage you. He's just a grinch."

Nick tucked the pastries into a glossy white bakery box and twirled around it a festive twine of red and green. He tied it with a flourish. As he handed the box across the counter to me, his fingers lightly brushed mine. I think he did that on purpose.

I handed over my credit card, and he rang it up, then we stood for a moment in awkward silence. I got the impression he was getting ready to say something when his gray eyes narrowed. His gaze slipped past my shoulder to the street outside.

I pivoted to find the source of his distraction. Chief Barnes was sauntering by, not in her usual imposing uniform but wrapped in a maroon puffer jacket with a fur-lined hood and matching fur boots. Her steely gaze pierced through the bakery window, zapping me with an intensity that could microwave popcorn.

Well, that ruined the Christmas-movie vibe.

I took a deep breath and turned back to Nick. "Thanks. You've got a knack for cookie counseling." I raised the box in a mock salute. Then, executing a casualness that should have won me an Oscar, I sauntered to the door, buying Barnes some time to amble past.

A casual glance over my shoulder confirmed that she'd moved on, her fur-trimmed figure swallowed by the snowflakes. With a sigh of relief, I plunged into the frosty air and headed in the opposite direction toward Rudolph's Reads and the book club meeting.

CHAPTER 11

Rudolph's Reads, in its festive grandeur, was prepared for the evening's book club meeting. Chairs were assembled into a cozy semicircle huddled near the warm fire. Hemingway had claimed his spot, snoring away blissfully in his plush cat bed. The glittering Christmas tree tucked in the corner sent a gentle reminder sparking through my brain. *Note to self: snag a tree for the inn tomorrow.*

As I stepped inside, familiar faces greeted me—Agnes, Doris, and Betty.

"Pastries!" Agnes exclaimed, her eyes gleaming mischievously as she beelined to me.

An eclectic mix of snacks was already spread out, but my pastries were treated like the crown jewel of the evening. Agnes found a platter and arranged them with almost reverential care. "I'm happy to see that you spent some more time with Nick, dear," she said.

Maggie, her eyes twinkling at the ongoing banter, drew me aside. "You didn't have to bring anything, but we appreciate the treats," she said, a genuine warmth in her voice. Our shared enthusiasm for the book spilled into our conversation.

We both agreed that Lucy, the canine police dog, stole every scene she was in. "Wait till you reach the end," Maggie gushed, her eyes lighting up with a secret delight. "You won't guess who the killer is!"

"Oh really?" I responded, my interest piqued. "I hope Lucy doesn't get hurt."

"Of course not. Lucy is fine. In fact, she's in the rest of the series, but I can't give any spoilers about the ending." Maggie just shook her head, a broad grin lighting up her face. "You'll have to find out for yourself."

It was an easy conversation, free of pretense and judgment. My heart warmed in a way that it hadn't in a long time. Since the fallout at my job and subsequent isolation, I had been lacking this simple comfort of companionship. I missed having friends. But here, with Maggie, I felt an easy connection, a potential friendship blooming.

Our conversation was invaded by Agnes, Doris, and Betty. Their voices, usually as subtle as a foghorn, were mysteriously hushed. I glanced around as they pulled us farther into the corner. No one else was paying attention—they were busy milling around the food table and having their own conversations.

"Have you made any progress in the investigation?" Agnes whispered, looking out into the room to ensure that no one was listening.

"Maybe." I told her about my visit with Simon and Miranda. "I think Simon was going to close the inn down because of mice."

"Really?" Doris whispered out of the side of her mouth while nodding and smiling at the guests across the room. "Is that why Ivy closed it down a few weeks ago?"

"I don't think so. She liked to take some time before the holidays to regroup. She always shut it down for a week or two," Betty said.

Agnes pursed her lips. "Kind of convenient for the killer that there were no guests to witness it, if you ask me."

"What about Miranda?" Maggie asked. She appeared just as eager as the other ladies to get in on the mystery.

"She's thinks George was always only interested in her. She seems a little crazy."

The four other women nodded. "She is. Now that Ivy is gone, of course, her chances are much better," Betty said.

"Yeah, very convenient for her," I said.

Agnes looped her arm through mine, her eyes sparkling mischievously. "Wait till you meet the rest of the suspects."

The next thirty minutes were a whirlwind of introductions. There was Donna, a birdlike woman with a pair of reading glasses perched precariously on her nose, and Leonard, an overbearing chap who had more hair in his ears than on his head. Then we had the twins, Tilly and Tally—confusingly similar names and maddeningly identical Christmas sweaters. And there was Desmond, a man who gave off the aura of a grumpy hedgehog.

Eliot, upon introduction, grimaced. "You inherited the inn? You need to review your property lines." He offered to show up with the plot plans the next day. A sinking feeling hit my stomach, but then again, he might have useful information. Hopefully, he hadn't just invited himself over so he could push me down the stairs.

Then there was Cecelia, looking like a Christmas

tree had thrown up on her. Garlands swished around her hem, and tiny ornaments on her sleeves jingled as she moved. Her condolences for Aunt Ivy were as insincere as her smile.

Betty announced the beginning of the meeting with the rustling of her knitting project. "We're missing Nora. She may be late."

"Is that the woman from the animal shelter?" A rock settled in my stomach. I was one step closer to handing Prancer over to his real family.

"Yes, she's very nice. You'll love her. She's had to go out of town on a family issue," Maggie said then turned to the group. "Shall we get started?"

As we settled into discussing the book, Hemingway zigzagged around us, obviously more interested in sniffing our plates than hearing our literary debate.

Between discussions of our book's red herrings and plot twists, I studied the suspects. Eliot, not as subtle as he thought, shot clandestine glances my way, but he seemed much too delicate for pushing someone down the stairs. I doubted he had the stomach for murder. Maybe they'd argued and it had turned physical and the deadly fall had been a horrible mistake.

Cecelia's fingers danced nervously around her

designer purse. Hemingway was interested in the purse, too, and had managed to snake a paw inside and pilfer a lipstick that he then batted under the couch.

Our discussion was interrupted by the door swinging wide. A whirlwind of a woman, around forty and brimming with earthy energy, breathlessly tumbled into the room. "I hope I'm not too late!" she huffed.

The scent of fresh hay clung to her denim jacket, a clear sign of a life intertwined with nature. Curly chestnut hair, disobedient to the ponytail it was bound in, framed a face that bore laugh lines in all the right places.

"We're winding down, but dive right in. Oh, and Nora, meet Annie, Ivy's great-niece and the new owner of the Yule Drop Inn," Maggie introduced us.

Nora's warm smile met mine as we shook hands. "Oh, thank goodness! You must be taking care of Burrito. I was so worried."

"Burrito?" I had no idea what she was talking about. Had my aunt been planning on having some sort of Mexican dinner? She usually only served breakfast.

Nora's eyes widened. "Yes. Ivy adopted him right before she fell. When I heard about her passing, I was worried about him but had to run out of town and couldn't check on him. If you inherited the inn, surely he was there with it—" Her sentence broke off, and she stared at me with concerned eyes.

"You mean the Chihuahua?" I glanced at Doris, Agnes, and Betty, who seemed just as confused as I was.

"Yes. Please tell me he's okay," Nora said.

"He's fine, but I thought he was a stray."

"Ivy never told us about adopting a dog," Agnes said.

Nora nodded and reached for a chocolate chip cookie. "She was planning on surprising you three. He came special from a shelter in Texas, and she saw his picture and fell in love. I guess she must have kept the secret pretty good if you guys didn't even have a clue."

"That must have been the surprise she mentioned the day we found her," Doris said sadly.

"I bet it was." Betty stopped clacking her knitting needles and her brow creased. "But that dog wasn't in the house when we found her."

"He must have gotten outside somehow. That's where Annie found him," Doris said.

My mind flashed back to finding Prancer in the show. He had looked skinny, like he hadn't been fed in a while. Had he been outside the whole time after

Aunt Ivy's death? Poor thing. That was over a week ago.

But then I had to ask myself, *How did he get outside?* There was only one way. He must have run out after the killer.

The next morning, I woke up with renewed energy. After the book club, I felt like I was fitting in with the town, and I was eager to tackle my to-do list to get the inn open. Best of all, Prancer didn't have another family, and I could keep him at the inn.

I opened my eyes to see Prancer's brown orbs staring at me. "Morning, Prancer," I murmured, rubbing the sleep from my eyes, "or is it Burrito?"

His answer came in the form of a flurry of wagging and sloppy morning-breath kisses. Dog breath, yech.

"All right, all right. Prancer, it is." Burrito would just remind me of food.

He responded with a happy bark before bounding off the bed. We made our way downstairs. The sinking feeling in the pit of my stomach was getting less and less each time I passed the spot where Aunt Ivy had died. I supposed that was a good thing, especially if I was going to stay on and run the inn.

Prancer, having a bladder the size of a thimble, was already waiting at the door, whining to be let out.

I opened the door, its hinges creaking in protest. The stubborn winter wind rushed in, hissing through the small opening and dislodging a piece of paper that had been stuck in the latch. It fluttered down to the ground in a lazy spiral.

I bent down, picking it up.

I unfolded it, and my eyes scanned the hand-written warning: "Back off or yule be next."

A chill, sharper than the winter wind outside, shot up my spine. *Yule, huh?* The misspelling seemed almost... deliberate. Hilarious. The killer thought he was a comedian.

My gaze swept the vicinity, a sense of violation intensifying the chill. Someone had been here in the night while I was sleeping. Creepy. Was it the killer? It had to be. But who? Who knew I was digging into Aunt Ivy's death?

Had it been Eliot? I peered at the path leading from his yard to mine. No fresh footprints. But then, he could have driven.

Miranda? She had seemed very disturbed when I'd

been in her store yesterday. The woman seemed to have a few Christmas bulbs loose. I wouldn't have put it past her to drive around town, leaving threatening notes.

What about Simon? He'd acted uncomfortable when I'd asked about his issues with Ivy.

Cecelia and Eliot had been at the book club meeting. They might have overheard me talking with Agnes, Doris, and Betty.

And there was someone else too. Chief Barnes. *But surely, the chief of police wouldn't leave threatening notes... right? Though she'd seemed a little... off.* As the thought flashed across my mind, I felt a cold breeze sweeping in. Prancer, done with his morning duties, barreled through the door, shattering my thoughts.

He raced toward the kitchen and his food bowl. With one last glance outside, I closed the door, being careful to make sure I turned the lock. I didn't need a note-leaving, aunt-killing neighbor to sneak in on me.

I fed Prancer and stared at the note some more. It had to be from the killer. There was one way to find out. I trotted upstairs to where I'd put the note I'd found in Ivy's pocket and compared the writing.

Their similarities were stark. Same exaggerated loops. Same daggerlike dots over the *i*'s. Same undercurrent of threat.

I set the notes aside. Was there any way I could get handwriting samples from the suspects? I would let my subconscious noodle away on that while I proceeded with my to-do list. The exterminator was due in two hours, and before he came, I wanted to finish filling out those forms for the permits and get a look at Aunt Ivy's books so I could get more familiar with how she ran the inn and kept track of the money.

Aunt Ivy's office was a tax accountant's dream... if your accounting prowess predated computers. Everything was neat and tidy and kept in ledgers.

In the middle of the room sat Ivy's desk, a sturdy, mahogany monster of a piece gleaming with polish and age. On its expansive surface sat a vintage green-shaded banker's lamp casting a warm, inviting glow on the stacks of neatly arranged papers.

The bookcases, matching the desk in their deep chestnut hue, lined the room like sentries, their shelves bowed under the weight of hardback novels and ledgers. The scent of aged paper and ink hung in the air, a testament to decades of recordkeeping.

The novels were all romances, the kind my aunt had loved so much. The ledgers themselves were a motley crew of hardcover tomes, their colors faded with time, bearing labels of the various years Aunt Ivy had been in business. The edges of their pages had softened, feeling familiar and comforting under my fingers as I leafed through them.

Underfoot, a plush oriental rug dampened the sounds of my footsteps, its intricate patterns in reds, blues, and golds worn and mellowed with the passage of time.

The high-backed chair, upholstered in a forest green leather, looked as inviting as it was functional. It swiveled with a little creak, adding a quaint charm to the quiet room. The seat cushion, softened from years of use, exhaled a puff of old air as I settled into it, adding a touch of coziness.

Among all this, a bulky computer hummed, a relic in its own right. Aunt Ivy wasn't totally without modern help in her business keeping. I was actually familiar with her guest-booking system on the computer, having helped her out before, but I knew she preferred to do the old-fashioned daily accounting in her ledger. I would change that, but for now, I needed to see what she had down already and try to balance her books.

A nails-on-hardwood tap dance announced Prancer's arrival. He needed his nails cut. Did Ivy have a veterinarian for him? I supposed I should call around. I would need his medical records and would develop a relationship with someone for his health care.

I lifted the first ledger, its leather cover cool and smooth under my fingers. Wait a minute—this one wasn't for the inn. The entries were too odd. I looked at the first page. It read, "Christmas Carol Karaoke Charity Contest." It sounded like one of the charity events. I picked up the next one—"Candy Cane Cotillion." Yet another trumpeted "North Pole Polka Party." They sure had a lot of charity events. Aunt Ivy must have kept the records for those. I made a mental note to return them to Geraldine when I brought my permit forms back to the town hall.

The fifth book was for the inn, and I settled in, smiling at Aunt Ivy's familiar writing as I went over her expenses and income. I'd have just enough time to get familiar, take a shower, and grab a leftover pastry before the exterminator came.

CHAPTER 13

"Doesn't look like a bad infestation." Dan Putney's voice, a strange mix of gravelly undertones and nasal New England twang, echoed from inside the kitchen cabinet where the upper half of his body was. As he conducted his inspection, Prancer was at his heels, sniffing around the kitchen corners with a serious, investigative air.

Dan emerged from the cabinet, dusted himself off, and looked around my kitchen with a satisfied nod. He was a tall, thin man with a weathered face and kind smile. "Probably just a wayward mouse that came in from the cold. Happens all the time." He shrugged. "No droppings or nests. I'll lay some humane traps outside, and you should be right as rain."

"Thanks."

Prancer, having finished his inspection, lay down and looked up at us, ears perked.

Handing over two tiny pieces of a torn check, he winked. "Found this too. Might be important."

I squinted at the fragments. The color was light green and I could only see a few letters and the number one. Was it $1,000? No, $10,000? More? What was it doing under there? I glanced in. "Where's the rest of it?"

Dan shrugged and bent to scratch Prancer behind his ears. "That's all that was in there. Why would anyone rip up a check?"

Good question. Had someone tried to pay off Aunt Ivy? I remembered Agnes, Doris, and Betty saying that Benjamin Thornton had kept pestering her to let him buy her land, and she kept refusing. Was the check from him? Or was it from the killer? Maybe he was the killer. Would any of the other suspects give Aunt Ivy a check?

"Your aunt kept a clean kitchen. No bugs, either."

"Thanks. What do I owe you?"

We settled up, and I saw him to the door, Prancer standing by my side, his head cocked as if bidding Dan goodbye.

Once he was gone, I dashed upstairs, the pieces of

check in hand, Prancer trailing behind me. I compared the pen strokes with my earlier finds, but I only had two little scraps of check with numbers and only a few letters on them, and it was impossible to tell if the same person who had written the notes had written the check.

The gravelly crunch of car tires outside caught my ear. A Lincoln pulled into the driveway. Eliot got out, clutching a set of big rolled-up plans. *Guess he didn't feel like using the path through the woods today.* Prancer's tail wagged at the prospect of company as we trotted downstairs to let Eliot in.

Opening the door, I welcomed Eliot with a forced smile and guided him through the living room, keeping an eye on his face as we passed the bottom of the stairs, where Aunt Ivy had met her untimely end. Nothing. Not even a twitch.

"Thank you for coming, Eliot."

"Er... you're welcome. I'd like to get this settled."

"Of course. Would you like a pastry?" I still had a few left from the ones Nick had brought over.

"No, thanks." He unrolled the plans with shaky hands, pointing out property lines. "It appears your aunt Ivy may have built a shed on my property."

Prancer sniffed around the table, clearly unimpressed when no treats came his way.

"Is that why you snuck over here through the woods the night she died?" I asked, trying my best to sound like a seasoned detective from one of my novels.

Eliot's eyes widened, and he let out a stifled yelp. My investigatory technique was obviously flawless.

"I wasn't here that night." His eyes shifted to the left.

Aha! Everyone knew that meant someone was lying.

"Oh really?" I drawled, one eyebrow raised. "And how do you know what night it was?"

"Ahh... everyone knows." He shrugged and tried to act casual.

That might be true, but I still knew he was lying. "So you deny coming through the woods and arguing with my aunt."

"Yes."

I leaned closer, putting on my best inquisitive gaze. "Then how do you explain the footprints leading from your property?"

"What are you accusing me of?"

"Nothing yet, but there are clearly footprints, and they lead straight from your house." I wasn't actually sure where they led, but where else could they go?

Eliot deflated and looked like he might cry.

"Okay, I was here the other night, but I never talked to Ivy."

Did he think I was born yesterday? "You expect me to believe that you trudged all the way here through the snow and then just went home? And why go walk through the woods unless you didn't want a witness to see your car?"

"I like walking through the woods for exercise and thought I might try to talk to your aunt about the property lines again." Eliot collapsed into a chair. "It seems she had a dispute with the previous owner and was carrying her grudge over to me."

"So you pushed her down the stairs?"

Prancer's bark sounded like a warning. Maybe I should listen to him. Here I was, accusing a killer. It wouldn't be too hard for Eliot to do away with me too. He'd already done it once, and there was that threatening note I'd found in the door. But Eliot didn't look up to the task.

"Like I told the police, I didn't push her. I came here, but Ivy wasn't alone. I could see into the kitchen from the back, and she had someone with her, and it looked like they were in a big argument. Then a snowstorm kicked up, so I turned and went back home."

Could he be telling the truth? It sure seemed that way.

"Who was with her?" Had she argued with George and he'd killed her? Maybe she broke up with him. She'd never mentioned him to me, so I didn't think there was any great romance going on.

"Benjamin Thornton, and he did not look happy with your aunt."

CHAPTER 14

I loaded the ledgers and permit forms into my truck and headed to the town hall. Could those ripped-up-check pieces have been from Benjamin Thornton?

He'd been persistent in trying to get Ivy to sell. I chuckled, picturing Aunt Ivy ripping up his check and throwing the pieces at him. My laughter was cut off as another image flashed in my mind—Benjamin Thornton, red-faced with fury, hurling Aunt Ivy down the stairs. But wait—Eliot had said he'd seen them in the kitchen. Why would Thornton have gone upstairs with Ivy?

I arrived at the town hall and dragged the ledgers out of my car. I barely noticed the festive decor in the grand entrance and quickly followed the maze of hall-ways to the permitting offices.

Simon's door was firmly closed. A helpful lady at a neighboring desk, wearing a smile as bright as her flowery blouse, looked up as I approached.

"Can I assist you, dear?" she chirped.

"I filled out some permitting forms for the Yule Drop Inn. I was going to return them to Simon." I glanced at his door.

"Oh, he's taken a few days off, but I can help you."

I handed over the forms. "And the mouse problem is taken care of, so you can remove that from your database."

"Mice?" The lady behind the desk peered at her screen, her glasses perched precariously on her nose. "There's nothing about rodents here."

My mind raced. Simon had mentioned contamina-tion of the four-footed variety. Mice? No, wait—could he have meant Prancer? But Aunt Ivy was keeping him a secret to surprise Agnes, Doris, and Betty. Only a few people knew about Prancer, including... the killer.

If there was nothing about rodents in the database, then I certainly didn't want something added.

"Did I say mice? I must have gotten confused. There are no mice." I crossed my fingers behind my back. Technically, I didn't have mice anymore, anyway.

She looked at me, perplexed but amused.

My mind was racing with images of Simon pushing Ivy down the stairs and writing those ominous notes. If only I could get a look at his handwriting. Maybe he signed some of the forms.

"How long until I can open? Is there a procedure or something? Will I get a copy of the signed forms?"

"We'll need a check, of course," she replied, typing away.

"Of course," I echoed, my mind still racing with possibilities.

"And then I would say, in a couple of days, you'll be good to go. Everything is set up from your aunt, so there's just a lot of name changing and so forth." She looked up at me with genuine sympathy. "I'm very sorry for your loss. Ivy was a good old gal."

I smiled and nodded, touched by her kindness. "Thanks. You'll let me know when I can open?"

"Let me just make sure I have your number," she said, reaching for a pen.

I gave her my phone number, my mind still reeling from the new clue as I tried to get a better look at the forms on her desk to see if I could see Simon's signature.

"All set, unless there is something else." She was

looking at me, her brow slightly furrowed. Was it that obvious that I was scanning her desk?

"That's it for now. Thank you very much." I turned away, my cheeks heating as I headed toward Geraldine's desk.

Geraldine glanced up, a warm smile spreading across her face. "I'm so glad you came back, dear. It turns out we do have a budget for some charity shindigs. Here's a list with the dates." She handed me a list of the upcoming holiday-themed events.

Rudolph's Reindeer Rumba night, the Great Fruitcake Fling, and Snowman Sculpture Showdown had potential, but I was pretty sure I didn't want to have anything to do with Santa's Speedo Sprint.

"Thanks. I'll check my calendar and get back to you. Speaking of charity events," I said, thumping my aunt's ledgers onto her desk with a dramatic thud, "I found these in Ivy's office."

"Oh, yes. Let's see..." She picked them up, names flowing from her lips like titles of rejected Hallmark movies. "Christmas Carol Karaoke Contest, Candy Cane Cotillion, North Pole Polka Party. Hmmm..." Her brows furrowed, and she looked up at me with the concern. "One is missing. The Elf Extravaganza."

"Oh. I'll look for it when I get home. My aunt had a lot of ledgers."

"Thank you, dear. Ivy was kind enough to balance the books for some of our charity events. She was so helpful."

"She was nice like that." I glanced down at the list again. "Well, I'll let you know about these and look for the ledger. Could you tell me where Benjamin Thornton's office is?"

Geraldine's face darkened. "He's over on Tinsel Drive. You can't miss the building. Has a sign with his name in giant letters."

CHAPTER 15

As I walked the short distance to Thornton's office, I thought about the ominous note I'd found in my door. The killer knew I was looking into Aunt Ivy's death. Were they following me right now? And what would they do if they thought I was continuing my investigation? I glanced around nervously to see if it looked like I was being followed.

From everything I'd heard about Benjamin Thornton, his office building was a reflection of his personality. A three-story monstrosity of marble and glass, it gleamed with an air of self-importance that was very much out of place in our little village. The lobby was no less grand, adorned with gold-framed paintings of landscapes probably painted by someone famous—or someone who wanted to be.

Outside his office, a receptionist stood sentinel. Her brown hair was cut in a perfect bob, and her face remained expressionless as I approached.

"Can I help you?" she asked, her voice dripping with the kind of enthusiasm reserved for reading tax codes.

I squared my shoulders. "I'd like to see Mr. Thornton."

"And do you have an appointment?" she inquired, eyes fixed on her computer screen.

"No, but it will only take a minute," I assured her.

"I'm sorry, you'll have to make an appointment," she replied, not even glancing up.

I leaned across the desk and lowered my voice to a conspiratorial whisper. "I'm sure he'll want to see me. I've recently inherited the Yule Drop Inn, and I heard my aunt was involved in a transaction with him."

Her interest flared, and she perked up but still looked at me with suspicion. She picked up the phone and talked in a low voice then looked back at me. "He'll see you, but just for a minute."

"A minute's all I need." I grinned, heading toward the imposing mahogany door of Thornton's office.

Benjamin Thornton's office was much as I expected. Mahogany everywhere and leather chairs so plush they practically invited you to take a nap. Even the air had the smell of money.

Thornton himself was a mountain of a man, in his midforties, with a presence that filled the room. His eyes held a gleam that screamed greed, and his build made me think, *Yep, he could've easily pushed my aunt.*

"Your aunt drove a hard bargain," he said, leaning back in his overcompensating chair.

I raised an eyebrow. "So you made a bargain to buy the property?" Surprise trickled into my voice. Aunt Ivy selling to him? I doubted it.

He smiled, a grin that was more business strategy than emotion. "Not in so many words. But I'm happy to negotiate with you."

I eyed his desk, my gaze falling on the top corner of a check that stuck out from a manila folder. Not green, though. Right, plan B, then. I'd have to ask some questions to trip him up.

"So you did make an offer to my aunt?" I asked.

"Lots of offers. She turned me down. But now that she's gone..." He let his voice trail off.

"I might sell... or not."

"Ivy would want you to sell," he insisted, his voice as smooth as whipped cream.

"I'm not sure about that, but there are some hurdles. Dealing with that Simon Knox is no joy."

Thornton wrinkled his nose. "Tell me about it."

"Did you know he wrote up a violation for Aunt Ivy's little Burrito?"

Thorton's frowned deepened. "That yappy little dog?"

Aha! He'd given himself away. Not very many people knew about Burrito, er... Prancer.

My eyes narrowed in suspicion. "How did you know Aunt Ivy had a dog?"

I wasn't sure what I expected. I thought maybe he'd break down and confess like on TV, but he didn't seem fazed at all.

Thornton met my gaze with an air of indifference, clearly not the type to break down and confess on the spot. "I met the dog when I was over there making one of my usual offers."

"And Ivy ripped your check up? That must have made you angry."

"Check? We never got that far." He shrugged, but his eyes flickered just a bit. "She did make me a bit angry."

"So angry you pushed her down the stairs?" I asked, expecting a forceful denial.

Instead, he just laughed. "Push her? No, not me."

"But you were there the night she died."

"Yes, I was," he said calmly. "But when I left, your aunt was very much alive."

I left the office, not knowing what to think. I hadn't expected him to admit he had been there that night. And he'd been so calm. Maybe he wasn't the killer. I mulled it over as I walked down the street. I still had plenty of suspects.

"Selling the inn?" The voice was unmistakable. Chief Liza Barnes. I jumped, spinning to find her eyes narrowing at me, suspicious as a cat eyeing a suspiciously twitchy mouse.

"What? Why do you ask that?" I stammered, feeling caught red-handed—even though I hadn't done anything wrong.

She nodded toward Thornton's building, her expression filled with accusation. "Why else would you be there unless you're snooping around your aunt's death again?"

"Snooping? Me? Never!" I declared, my voice rising an octave in feigned innocence. "You said it was an accident."

Her gaze flicked to the glass building, like she expected it to confess something. "Anyway, he has an alibi."

I snorted. "An alibi? Huh, hardly. Someone saw him in the house!"

She raised an eyebrow, clearly unimpressed. "At the exact time of death?"

"I have to admit I don't know exactly when that was," I said, feeling my bravado deflate.

"Er... right, so stop messing around," she snapped, stomping off after fixing me with a glare that could curdle milk.

I watched her leave, my mind awhirl. So she had investigated it as more than an accident. That was interesting. But why was she pretending like it was one? Thinking about the notes, I wondered if Barnes's handwriting had the same exaggerated loops and daggerlike dots. That was silly, though. Why would Barnes want to kill my aunt?

CHAPTER 16

"Means, motive, and opportunity. That's what you need to consider," Agnes announced, taking a bite of her grilled cheese sandwich. Cheese oozed out onto her plate.

I'd spotted Agnes, Doris, and Betty in Jingle Bell Java after my encounter with Barnes. They'd waved me in, and I now sat at their table, sipping a mug of cocoa and nibbling a gigantic gingerbread cookie as I filled them in on the latest events regarding Aunt Ivy's murder —the threatening note I'd found in the door, my visit to Thornton, and running into Barnes.

Betty unraveled a row of her knitting, her eyebrows mashing together in thought. "Thornton's motive is as clear as this yarn is tangled."

"But Barnes said he had an alibi," Doris chimed in.

"Why was Barnes checking alibis?" Agnes asked.

Doris shrugged. "Maybe that was before she ruled it an accident."

"What about Eliot? He was there that night," I pondered, nibbling on the cookie's leg.

"He seems too timid for murder," Betty mused.

"Those timid ones are always the killers!" Agnes exclaimed, waving her sandwich for emphasis.

"There's still Miranda Hightower. I could totally picture her doing it," I added, my mind racing with images of Miranda's ginormous necklace glinting in the light as she shoved my aunt down the stairs.

"And don't forget Cecelia Rothschild. We still don't know what they even fought about," Doris said, her eyes wide with intrigue.

My thoughts wandered to Simon Knox. "Simon knew about Prancer. He wrote up a code violation for animals, which I thought was for mice, but it turns out he never put that into the system. Anyone who knew about Prancer would have to have been at Ivy's house because she was keeping him a secret."

Betty looked up from her knitting. "Why would Simon want to kill Ivy?"

The table went silent for a moment, each of us lost in thought.

"What about the torn check pieces the extermi-nator found?" I asked.

"That could be from anything. Might not even be related to the murder," Betty said with a shrug, her eyes lost in her knitting.

"It could be from a payoff or bribe," Doris added, her voice tinged with a knowing wisdom that only years of soap-opera watching could provide.

We all fell into silence again as we sifted through the suspects.

"I know what you need to do!" Agnes suddenly exclaimed, nearly causing me to jump out of my seat. Her eyes sparkled with excitement. "You need a grand opening party where we invite all the suspects."

"Party?" I choked out. I wasn't quite ready to open the inn yet. But I had to admit, it wasn't a bad idea. I had an image of myself revealing the killer, like Columbo except with a more stylish raincoat.

"You need to do something to celebrate your new ownership," Doris said. "When were you planning on opening?"

"They said all the permits should be signed off in a few days, and I suppose I need to open sooner than later." I needed to get money flowing in.

"Ivy always liked to reopen three weeks before

Christmas. Said she got the most bookings then," Agnes said.

"A party would be good as a trial run. I'll wear my silver outfit." Doris's eyes got hazy like she was mentally rummaging through her closet for matching shoes and purse.

"I really could use a trial run with the breakfast. I know Ivy's customers loved her breakfasts," I said, my voice trailing off as I considered the mountain of tasks ahead. Decorating, cooking—I hadn't even started.

"Oh, you can practice on us. Tomorrow morning!" Agnes declared, her face glowing with the anticipation of being my culinary guinea pig.

I could only nod, feeling both excited and overwhelmed. *Guess I'd better take another look at my to-do list and review my breakfast recipes.*

WITH AN ARMFUL of groceries and a heart full of anticipation, I pushed open the front door to the inn, pausing to scan the entryway for any more threatening notes. Thankfully, there were none.

"Prancer!" I called, kicking off my shoes. The sound of tiny nails clicking against the hardwood floor filled the air as the little dog bounded into the hall.

I chuckled, greeting him with a pat on the head. "I got you some treats."

Prancer's tail wagged, his tongue lolling out in a canine grin as if he understood me. Together, we made our way into the kitchen.

I found the box of treats and tossed one to Prancer. He caught it before it hit the floor. I unloaded my groceries onto the wooden countertop. Among the fresh fruits, eggs, and butter, a sense of nostalgia settled in the room. I'd spent many mornings in my great-aunt Ivy's kitchen, helping her with breakfast.

I pulled out Ivy's old recipe book, its pages worn and stained from years of use. As I flipped through it, memories flooded back. Pancakes, quiches, muffins— each page a tribute to her mastery of breakfast.

Prancer settled beside my chair, his eyes fixed on the book as if he, too, was considering the recipes. He let out a soft whine, his eyes darting between me and the pages.

"You miss Ivy, too, huh?" I asked, smiling down at him. She'd only had him a short while, but anyone who knew Aunt Ivy for even just a few hours loved her. Why would Prancer be any different?

I settled on a few recipes that seemed delicious and which I had ingredients for—Ivy's famous blueberry muffins, a fluffy cheese omelet, and her renowned cinnamon-apple pancakes.

As I ran around double-checking pans and ingredients, Prancer's eyes followed my every move. There was a strange intensity in his gaze, something beyond the usual canine curiosity.

"You're acting like you've got a secret recipe of your own," I said, laughing. But as I looked into Prancer's eyes, a thought struck me. "Of course you do. You were here when Ivy died."

Prancer's ears perked up, his eyes widening. He gave a soft, affirmative bark.

I felt a chill run down my spine. "You know who did it, don't you? If only you could talk."

Prancer titled his head and gave a soft woof.

With a smile, I reached down and gave him a gentle pat. "Don't worry, my little witness. I'm going to figure this out if it's the last thing I do."

CHAPTER 17

"This is delicious!" Agnes declared, holding up a fork of fluffy eggs before shoving it into her mouth with unbridled enthusiasm.

I grinned, flipping a pancake. "Thanks. Save room for Ivy's cinnamon-apple pancakes."

Doris, Agnes, and Betty perched at the kitchen table, the picture of a grandmotherly taste-test panel. They nibbled on my blueberry muffins, comparing them to Ivy's creations.

"Needs more blueberries," Agnes declared as if judging a gourmet cooking show.

"The omelet's perfect, though," Betty chirped, her eyes twinkling. She forked another fluffy bite into her mouth, her knitting needles momentarily forgotten.

"And these pancakes?" Doris inquired, drenching

hers in syrup. "Divine, but maybe a splash more syrup next time?"

I laughed. "A splash more? I'll need to invest in a syrup company at the rate you use it."

Prancer was enjoying himself, too, as he pranced around, successfully begging a tidbit from each lady.

Agnes, her mouth still full, managed to say, "Watched *Murder She Wrote* last night. The compelling motives are always greed, jealousy, and revenge." She winked, turning our breakfast into a murder investigation.

"Greed could certainly be Benjamin's game," I said, serving up another stack of pancakes.

Agnes forked a pancake and grinned. "What about Eliot? He fought with Ivy over that property line."

Doris frowned thoughtfully. "But maybe that was more about revenge. He didn't like that the shed was built over the line."

Betty forked up more eggs. "But that happened before he even owned it."

"He's a strange one, but I still feel like he might be telling the truth about not even coming in that night. Benjamin did admit to being here too." I sat down and stirred my coffee.

Doris snuck a piece of pancake to Prancer under

the table. "What about Miranda? Pure jealousy if you ask me."

Agnes nodded, dramatically clutching her chest. "That woman could give envy a bad name. If jealousy were a sport, she'd be an Olympic champion."

"And then there's Cecelia," I mused, leaning back in my chair, tapping a finger on my chin. "Now, she's the wild card. What's her motive?"

"Cecelia's like one of those weird mystery ingredients on a cooking show," Betty said, clicking her knitting needles. "Could be sweet, could be sour. Nobody knows until you taste it."

"Or in this case, until she spills the beans," Agnes added, winking. "Which we're hoping the killer will do at your grand opening party. Have you thought more about that?"

"Yes. In fact, I already made a list of what I need to decorate. I was thinking of getting a big, tall balsam fir like Aunt Ivy always got. Is Tinsel Tree Farm still a good place to buy?"

"The best." Betty stood, took her plate to the sink, and started washing it.

"I'll go there, then."

"What time would that be, about?" Agnes asked, handing Betty her plate and opening the dishwasher.

"What time?" I looked at Agnes suspiciously. Why

would she want to know that?

"Yes, dear. They get fresh trees at one p.m. today," Agnes said.

"Oh! Guess I'll go around two, then."

"Perfect!" Agnes put the last of the dishes into the dishwasher. "Now, what are you planning for food? Where will you set things up?"

"Ivy always had parties in the big living room and spilling into the dining room. Let's go take a look." Doris jumped up from her chair, and we all headed toward the living room.

"I think you should put the Christmas tree right there by the staircase. Ivy always had it there," Agnes said as we all avoided looking at the bottom of the stairs.

Betty pointed toward the corner. "A buffet table would look grand there. It would be like Ivy's traditional holiday feasts but with a modern twist to kick off the new ownership."

"Oh, I like that," I said, already picturing it. "We could have trays of mini quiches, assorted pastries, and then some warm appetizers."

"Don't forget the coffee station!" Doris added. "People will want to mingle and chat."

"And hopefully, spill some of their secrets," Betty said.

"Speaking of that, we'll need some festive cock-tails," Agnes said, clapping her hands together. "Something with a bit of zing to get tongues wagging."

"And a nonalcoholic punch for those of us who should keep our tongues under control," Doris added, giving Agnes a knowing glance.

The ideas continued to flow as we discussed menu items and holiday decor, such as napkins and tablecloths.

"Don't forget the mistletoe," Betty said with a wink. "It's not a Christmas party without some unexpected romance."

"Or unexpected embarrassment," I said, thinking of my own history with mistletoe mishaps.

"Oh, come on," Agnes said, nudging me. "You never know who you might run into under there. You could order some desserts from Nick if you don't have time to make it all yourself."

That wasn't a bad idea. His pastries were divine, and I would have to hire out some of the catering. I was, however, not going to get anywhere near any mistletoe with Nick around.

The planning continued, with each of us taking on tasks and bringing the grand opening party to life in our minds. Prancer woofed his approval as we settled on the final plans.

CHAPTER 18

By two-thirty that afternoon, I'd picked up some supplies for the party, made a to-do list, and bought the biggest tree I could find over at the tree lot. That was how I found myself in the snow-covered, pine-scented parking lot of the Tinsel Tree Farm, staring at a seven-foot-tall tree. My eyebrows scrunched together as I wondered how I could best wrangle this giant piece of nature onto my truck without making a spectacle of myself.

First, I attempted a sideways hug, thinking I could just shimmy it over. Nope. The tree gave me a scratchy embrace back. Then I thought, *What if I roll it?* Halfway through the roll, I realized trees weren't meant to be rolled, and I ended up tangled in the branches, one leg in the air like a deranged ballerina.

"Can I help you?" a voice called out, thick with amusement.

Shoot. That voice sounded familiar. I peeked out from between the pine branches covering my eyes. It was Nick.

"Oh, hi there," I said. My cheeks flushed, matching the festive ornaments scattered around the lot. "I was just, you know, making sure the tree looked good from all angles."

Nick's eyes crinkled as he grinned, approaching me. "Well, it seems to be checking you out from all angles too. Let me help you."

With practiced ease, he helped untangle me from the tree's enthusiastic grasp and effortlessly lifted it onto my truck.

Nick and I worked together to secure the tree onto the truck, the ropes seemingly with minds of their own as they tangled and twisted. Finally, after what felt like an epic battle, we had the tree strapped down and secure.

"I guess it was good luck running into you here. Are you getting a tree too?" I asked, wiping my brow and glancing at Nick, who was expertly tying the last knot.

Nicks eyes narrowed. "No, Gram suddenly decided she needed some pine boughs."

We looked at each other suspiciously over the roof of the truck, the unspoken questions lingering in the crisp winter air. Had Agnes done that on purpose so we'd run into each other? And was I glad about that or not?

"You need help getting this tree into the inn?" Nick finally asked, breaking the silence.

"I'm sure I can manage on my own," I said, flexing my arms dramatically.

Nick laughed, a warm, rich sound that resonated in the stillness. "From what I've seen, you do have quite a way with trees, but I have a box of day-old éclairs in my truck. If you promise to make some of your aunt Ivy's famous hot chocolate, I'll share them with you and help you get the tree into the inn."

Éclairs? How could I say no. "My friend, you've got yourself a deal."

NICK FOLLOWED me back to the inn, and we wrestled the tree inside without incident. The branches fell into place with what I imagined was the satisfied sigh of a tree finally settling into its home for Christmas. The room filled with the heady scent of pine, making me momentarily dizzy.

Prancer dashed around us, barking his approval, tail wagging furiously. Nick bent down to pet him, and I could have sworn Prancer's grin matched Nick's. "He's a character, isn't he?" Nick said, ruffling Prancer's ears.

"Indeed, and a critic. Let's see if your éclairs pass his taste test," I teased, leading the way to the kitchen.

Nick's eyes twinkled. "That's a challenge, Miss Winters."

I pulled out Aunt Ivy's cocoa recipe and snatched it away when Nick tried to look over my shoulder. "No peeking! It's got a secret ingredient that's been passed down for generations."

He laughed. "I'll just unbox the éclairs. Got a plate?"

We settled in the living room, the éclairs strategically placed between us and dessert plates in our laps. I bit into one, the rich chocolate glaze mingling with the soft, creamy inside. Heaven, pure heaven.

"This is delicious," I said, trying not to moan inappropriately.

Nick looked amused, his eyes crinkling at the corners. "I can see that."

"What?"

He pointed to the corner of his lip, and I swiped at mine with a napkin, discovering a dollop of chocolate glaze. My cheeks warmed, but Nick didn't notice. He'd already stood and was looking at the boxes of ornaments that I'd lugged from the storage room earlier.

"These look great. Want some help decorating?" Nick asked, his eyes sparkling with genuine interest.

I looked at him askance. None of the guys I'd ever dated liked decorating the tree. "Are you serious?"

"Of course! I love decorating. Gram and I look forward to it every year," he replied, his grin widening.

My eyes narrowed suspiciously. A man who liked decorating? Did he have an ulterior motive? This was new territory for me, but I decided to plunge into it, curiosity piqued.

We proceeded to decorate. As I handed Nick some of Aunt Ivy's antique ornaments, he held them up to the light, appreciating the intricate designs, the sparkling gems, and the well-aged gold leaf. I found myself watching him more than the ornaments, intrigued by his delicate handling of each piece.

He dug into the garland next, eyes widening. "She's got almost every color—red, green, gold, and silver."

"That's only four colors, really. It comes in more," I said in Ivy's defense, feigning a stern look.

Nick chuckled. "Well, maybe Ivy liked to keep things simple."

That was when Prancer decided to join the fun,

barking happily, grabbing the garland, and dragging it around like a toy. I rushed to save Ivy's cherished decorations.

"He's a handful," Nick said. "Gram said there was something unusual about you finding him?"

I told Nick how I'd found Prancer out in the snow, mistakenly thinking he was a baby deer, thanks to some realistic antlers.

Nick laughed, his deep chuckle resonating in the room. "A baby deer? Deer are much bigger than this little guy."

"I know that now, but I'm from the city. Never saw a deer before. Of course, the garland on his antlers might have been a clue."

"Garland?"

"Aunt Ivy must have been dressing him up for Christmas." My smile faltered. "She'd adopted him the week before but was keeping him a secret. I guess she was going to show him off to your gram, Doris, and Betty the morning after she was killed. I didn't know that she'd named him Burrito."

"Burrito?" Nick tilted his head to look at the dog. "He looks more like a Prancer to me."

"Me too. Anyway, he must have been here the night my aunt was killed. I think maybe he ran out after the killer."

Nick's expression turned to concern. "So about this unofficial murder investigation of yours... what's going on? Gram said you were helping her look into the murder. I hope you guys aren't doing anything dangerous."

I tried to keep the amusement out of my expression. It sounded like Agnes thought she was playing a much bigger role in this investigation than she was. But I didn't want to burst her bubble.

I waved away his concern. I decided I wouldn't tell him about the threatening note I'd found in the door. I leaned back, channeling my inner Hercule Poirot, minus the mustache. Well, hopefully, I didn't have a mustache from the éclair frosting. I wiped my lip just in case.

"We have a bunch of suspects, and the exterminator found some pieces of a ripped-up check under the cabinet." I told him about our suspects and their potential motives.

Nick's brow shot up. "Interesting."

"That's not all," I said, warming to my role as amateur detective. "Benjamin Thornton is practically foaming at the mouth to buy the inn, and Eliot saw him here the night Ivy died."

Nick looked thoughtful. "That means Eliot was here, too, then."

"He was, but he claims he never came inside. He saw Ivy and Benjamin arguing."

"That seems suspicious," Nick noted, his eyes narrowing.

I shrugged. "Sure, but Chief Barnes says Thornton has an alibi." I glanced up at Nick. His face hardened.

"Barnes is pretty good, so if she says he has one, then it's probably true."

Nick was praising his ex. It sounded like maybe they were still friends... or more?

"Your grandmother has been having a good time playing amateur sleuth. She even has a list of motives," I said, my voice tinged with a hint of mystery. "There's greed, jealousy, revenge... and she has suspects to go with them."

Nick's eyebrows shot up. "Speaking of greed, I had another run-in with Simon. I swear he's gearing up to ask for a payoff."

My eyes widened. "Payoff? Like bribery?"

"Yeah. I've heard from other businesses that he takes bribes to go easy on the violations, or he threatens to make some up if you don't pay."

I tapped my chin, feeling the first tingles of a new idea. "Wait a minute. What if the check was Aunt Ivy's payoff?"

"Why rip it up, then?"

Good point. The conversation turned to the upcoming town festivities, but the whole time, I kept thinking about those check pieces and the threatening notes.

After Nick left, I dashed up to look at the checkbook for the inn. The checks weren't green. I was back to square one.

CHAPTER 19

*L*eft alone in the cozy little office at the inn, I found myself knee-deep in suspects and a to-do list that looked suspiciously like my aunt Ivy's infamous Christmas cookie recipe—long and complex.

George? No, too nice, too heartbroken. But wait... didn't they usually say it was the boyfriend or husband? That was certainly true with most of the cases at the old law firm.

Miranda? Crazy enough to make a rabbit stew without the stew part. But she was almost too crazy to have orchestrated something like this. I thought about the threatening note I'd found in the door. That had been the morning after I'd visited Baubles and Boughs and asked questions about Ivy.

I remembered the gaudy earrings I'd bought. I'd shoved the bag in my closet without even taking them out.

I dashed upstairs and yanked open the closet. There was the bag crumpled in the corner. Inside was a receipt with Miranda's flamboyant "Thank you!" sprawled across it. Aha! It was loopy, just like the threatening notes.

I pulled the notes from my drawer and held them up to compare. Similar? Yes. Exact? I couldn't be sure, and from what I'd learned at the firm, handwriting comparisons really did require an expert.

It didn't guarantee that she was the killer, but it also didn't rule her out.

I needed more intel on Cecelia. I hadn't had much of a chance to talk to her at the book club. How could I find a way to spend some time with her? My eyes fell on the list of upcoming charity events. Beside the event was the name of the committee member in charge. Cecelia's name popped up not once but twice—the Rudolph's Reindeer Rumba and the Snowman Sculpture Showdown. Both sounded festive, but a rumba with reindeer seemed dangerous. Besides, I couldn't even lead in a two-step.

Snowman Sculpture, though? Now, that seemed

more my style. Snow, ice, cold fingers, and carrot noses.

I grinned, envisioning the plan. I could volunteer, look altruistic, and gently interrogate Cecelia, all without breaking a sweat. Well, you didn't usually sweat in twenty-degree temperatures anyway.

As if the universe had overheard my private musings, my phone rang, and the town hall's number flashed on the screen. "This is Annie," I answered, trying to sound like a professional business owner and not the flustered new innkeeper I was.

"Annie, this is Geraldine down at the town hall. All your permits are approved to open the inn. You can come get them anytime."

I cheered inwardly. "That's great. I was thinking about coming down and volunteering for one of the charities anyway."

"Great, which one?" Geraldine asked, her voice accompanied by a rustle of papers.

"The Snowman Sculpture Showdown."

"Oh, that one is meeting tonight!" Geraldine chirped.

"Perfect!" I replied, trying not to sound too eager. The sooner I could interrogate Cecelia, the better. Hopefully, she'd write something down, and I could check out her handwriting.

"I'll let Cecelia know you'll be there. Seven o'clock at the church basement."

Great. I was going to meet my aunt's potential killer in a creepy church basement. I could hardly wait.

"We're open until seven tonight if you want to pick up the permits. Don't forget to bring a check! Oh, and did you find the ledger for the Elf Extravaganza? If you did, please bring it."

Oops, I'd forgotten to look for that.

"Will do, Geraldine," I promised.

I HURRIED through the maze of hallways in the town hall, surrounded by the smell of aged wood and bureaucracy. Now that I had my permits, I was eager to get the plans for the grand reopening party in place and start to get some guests. I'd reopened the listing online and had already anxiously checked my phone a dozen times on the way to town to see if anyone had booked a room.

Geraldine was sitting at her usual desk. Simon's door was closed. Was he in there, hatching up another blackmail scheme?

"Annie!" Geraldine waved me over. "Here for the inn permits, right?"

"That's right," I replied, hoping the process would be smooth.

"Good, good." She looked up over the rim of her glasses. "You've got the check?"

"Yes, of course," I answered, handing it over. "Everything's in order, I hope?"

"Oh, yes," she said, taking the check and putting it into a deposit bag. "It's just that things have been so busy lately, and I need to get these deposits in."

"I understand," I said, offering a sympathetic smile.

"Did you happen to find that ledger?" she asked.

I'd done a cursory search before coming downtown but it didn't turn up. "Not yet. I'll keep looking."

"Thank you. I'm sure it will turn up." Geraldine picked up some papers from her desk. "Now, here are your permits, dear. Everything looks perfect."

I took the permits, feeling a sense of accomplishment. "So the inn is mine to open?"

"Absolutely," she confirmed. "Good luck. I'm sure you'll do as good a job as Ivy did."

I left the Town Hall, feeling both excited and nervous. What if I didn't do as good a job as Ivy? What if no one booked a room? What if they did and gave me bad reviews?

I didn't have much of a choice, though. I couldn't go back to paralegal work now.

With the precious permits secured safely in my bag, I trotted over to Snowflake Stationery, the most charming little shop you'd ever seen. The window display was full of festive holiday decorations, and the scent of cinnamon candles wafted out as I opened the door.

"Good afternoon!" A teen with short blue-tipped hair greeted me cheerfully.

"Afternoon. I'm looking for invitations," I said. "I'm reopening the Yule Drop Inn, and I need something that screams Yule Notch chic but whispers affordable."

The girl laughed and guided me to a collection that was both elegant and budget friendly.

I scanned the selection. Cards with frosted trees, whimsical reindeer, and twinkling stars vied for my attention. But it was the snowflakes that caught my eye, each one delicately unique, just like Aunt Ivy used to say about people. I found a card adorned with a shimmering snowflake design, its intricate patterns sparkling with hints of silver and blue. The paper itself was textured, giving a tactile dimension to the frosty design, as if the snowflake could melt right off the page.

With invitations in hand, I stepped back out into the wintry streets of Yule Notch. Glancing across the way, I noticed Rudolph's Reads was still open. The warm glow of its lights beckoned me, and I realized I had time to spare before the snowman-charity-event meeting.

The bell jingled merrily as I pushed open the bookstore door. Hemingway glanced up from his perch by the crackling fire, his green eyes narrowing in what I chose to interpret as a greeting.

"Hey, Annie, how's it going?" Maggie's voice rang out from behind the counter, where she was expertly wrapping a stack of books in festive paper.

"I just wanted to drop by and personally invite you to the inn's opening party," I said, smiling. I held out one of the snowflake invitations that I'd managed to fill out on my way over.

Maggie's eyes lit up as she took the invitation, examining the delicate design. "Oh, it's just lovely! I wouldn't miss it for the world."

Hemingway, evidently sensing that a social gathering was in progress, lumbered over, his tail twitching with feline grace. He settled at our feet, purring loudly.

"Why don't you join me for some tea?" Maggie offered, motioning to the plump armchairs in front of the fire. "I just got in some new mysteries that you might find intriguing."

"Great timing. I finished the one I bought last time. It was great." I followed her to the seating area. As we sipped tea, Hemingway made himself comfortable on my lap, demanding attention with a gentle nudge of his head.

Maggie's eyes darted around the store, ensuring that we were alone. She leaned closer, her voice dropping to a conspiratorial whisper. "So, what's been going on with the investigation into your aunt's death?"

I blew out a breath and then filled her in on all the happenings since I'd last talked to her at the book club. "I'm really no closer to figuring out who killed my aunt, but I'm now positive it was not an accident."

Maggie nodded and sipped her tea. "You need to talk to the suspects, find out what they have for alibis. Just like in the mystery novels."

"I do, but since I'm new in town, that makes it rather difficult. The grand reopening party was actually your grandmother's idea, along with Agnes and Betty of course. They think it might flush out the killer."

Maggie's eyes sparkled with a mixture of pride and amusement. "Trust Gram to come up with such a scheme! Those three are always up to something."

"I've noticed. But it's a good idea. And I'm actually on my way to the committee meeting for the Snowman Sculpture Showdown charity event."

"You're on the committee? Those can be fun. I served on the North Pole Polka Party committee. If I never hear accordion music again, it will be too soon." Maggie laughed. "Your aunt was always big on the charity events."

I sighed. "I know, and I want to carry that on, but..." I leaned closer and wiggled my brows. "I have an ulterior motive."

"Oh?" Maggie leaned in, too, her interest piqued.

"One of the suspects, Cecelia Rothschild, is heading the committee. It'll give me a chance to find out more about her and the argument she had with my aunt."

From his perch by the fire, Hemingway lifted his head as if suddenly interested in our conspiracy. His green eyes seemed to approve.

Maggie's eyes widened, then she grinned. "Oh well —you won't be alone. Gram is on that committee too."

We spent the next ten minutes finishing our tea and getting to know each other better. As I left

Rudolph's Reads, I felt lighter, clutching my new books and cherishing the feeling that, in Maggie, I'd found a new friend. Even Hemingway escorted me to the door as if bidding me goodbye.

I turned away from the warmth of the bookstore and wrapped my scarf around the lower part of my face. The prospect of the Snowman Sculpture Showdown committee meeting didn't seem nearly as cozy as spending time in the bookstore.

CHAPTER 20

The utilitarian church basement seemed almost out of place in the festive town of Yule Notch. Its overhead fluorescent lighting buzzed monotonously, casting a sterile glow on metal folding chairs and the manila-and-green-tile floor. There was a distinct smell in the air, a bit moldy with an undertone of earthy incense.

As I descended the stairs, a strange mix of anticipation and nervousness twisted in my stomach. Today was all about subtlety. My goal was to get something—anything—about Cecelia's alibi for the night Aunt Ivy died, without arousing suspicion.

"Annie! It's lovely to see you here!" called a tall woman with wispy gray hair. I remembered meeting her a few times when I'd visited my aunt. She was

Martha, a local schoolteacher with a soft spot for knitting. "I heard about the inn reopening. We've all missed it so."

"Thanks, Martha!" I grinned. "I'm hoping to make it a hub for the community again. Speaking of which, you're invited to the grand reopening party this Friday."

Martha clapped her hands, her glasses bouncing on her nose. "Splendid! I wouldn't miss it for the world."

Around the room, other townsfolk began to gather. There was Bill, the portly butcher, who never seemed to be without his white apron; Nora, who I'd met at the book club; and several others, all bubbling with excitement and curiosity about the inn's return.

As I was introduced and welcomed, I scanned the room for Cecelia, finally spotting her at the front, arranging papers. She was wearing a bright-green dress with sparkles and silver garland-like froufrous on the sleeves. Did she always dress so flamboyantly? It was probably some new designer line that I was unaware of.

Doris sidled up to me. "You here to scope out the suspects?" she whispered, giving Cecelia the side-eye.

"Something like that," I mumbled out of the side of my mouth.

Cecelia's voice rang out, pulling us into the meeting. Darn, I hadn't had a chance to interrogate her yet. I'd even thought up a way to try to trip her up. Thankfully, there was a table of coffee and pastries being guarded by a pinched-nosed woman, which must have been for after. Maybe I could corner Cecelia then.

"Ladies and gentlemen, thank you for coming. We have a lot to cover for the Snowman Sculpture Showdown. It's going to be our biggest event yet!"

We took our seats, and she detailed the plan: an outdoor competition held in the town square, where teams would craft snowmen. Prizes would be awarded, local businesses would set up stalls, and all proceeds would go to charity.

Then came the task assignments. "Martha, you'll handle the judges' booth. Bill, we need you at the food station."

When it came to me, Cecelia smiled. "Annie, you can be the waste-management coordinator."

A titter ran through the room.

I frowned. "What exactly does the waste-management coordinator do?"

Cecelia gave me a patronizing smile. "It's the most important task. You'll be in charge of making sure the town common is cleaned after the event's activities each day. Picking up litter, disposing of leftover snow and materials, and general tidying of the town square. It's the sort of task that everyone appreciates but no one wants to do, particularly after a long, cold day outside."

That didn't sound so bad. "Okay, great."

The meeting wound down, and folks made a beeline for the refreshment table. I joined them, trying to position myself so that I could strike up a conversation with Cecelia. I loaded my plate with chocolate chip cookies and a Danish. They definitely were not as delicious looking as Nick's. Probably from the grocery store.

Just as I'd managed to get next to Cecelia, Nora approached me. "Annie, how's Burrito? Doing well?"

Before I could answer, Cecelia's sharp voice cut in. "Those little Chihuahuas are nothing but dangerous ankle biters!"

Nora and I stared at her. Cecelia's cheeks flushed, and she quickly tried to cover her outburst. "I mean, they can be a handful sometimes."

Nora's eyes narrowed, but she said nothing.

"I named him Prancer, and he's doing fine," I said.

"That's great. Oh, I need a coffee." Nora made a beeline for the coffee urn.

Cecelia reached past me for a cream puff. "It's nice

to see you taking over for your aunt with the charity involvement."

"I'm trying to fill in some of the gaps she left. But I can't do the accounting like she did. Did you help her with the ledgers?" I asked.

She frowned. "Whyever would you ask that?"

"I just thought... I mean, we can't find one of them, and I was hoping you had it if you shared that task with her."

Cecelia shook her head. "I'm not one for numbers, I'm afraid."

"I see. That didn't have anything to do with your falling-out that you had with Ivy, did it?"

"Falling-out? Who told you there was a falling-out?" She put another cream puff on her plate.

I shrugged. "Oh, I just heard. But you made up, right? Is that why you were at her house that night?"

Cecelia's eyes narrowed to slits, and she glanced around, leaning closer.

"What are you trying to insinuate?" she hissed. "I wasn't at the inn that night, but if you're playing detective, why not look to George McKinley? He was very angry that your aunt didn't return his affections. I saw him leaving the inn just after ten p.m. I was driving past on my way to the Starlight Observatory." She ended with a warning look and scurried off to the coffee urn, leaving me to ponder her words.

"Wait, what?" I muttered. George had told me he wasn't there that night. Had he lied? And why were so many people at the inn? Eliot, Benjamin, Cecelia, George—it was starting to feel like a town meeting.

Doris stepped up beside me. "Did you get anything good?" she whispered.

"Maybe," I replied, the cogs still turning.

"Me and the gals were talking about stopping over at the inn to discuss our strategy for the party. How's tomorrow right before noon?"

"Perfect. I have invitations for you guys for the party too. And I can fill you in on anything new then."

"Thornton's alibi checks out," Betty announced with an air of finality, pausing to take a bite of her croissant. I could almost taste the flaky buttery layers myself.

It was eleven o'clock in the morning, and the three ladies had burst through the door like clockwork. Agnes had brought pastries from Mistle Dough Bakery and arranged them on a plate as if they were gold bars.

We were seated at the kitchen table with steaming coffees. Prancer pranced around at our feet, anxiously watching for falling crumbs.

It was a welcome break from my busy morning, which I had spent embroiled in party logistics, grappling with addresses, invitations, catering, and the

Herculean task of pulling off a grand bash on short notice.

"How do you know?" Doris asked, eyeing a pistachio scone.

"I found out he was at the elementary school, setting up the emergency shelter. Remember we were supposed to have that big storm but it fizzled out?" Betty replied, her words coming out in crumbs.

"That's right. It seemed like it was going to be a doozy, but by morning, it was all over," Agnes added.

I remembered what Eliot had said about the snow starting when he saw Thornton. Someone had killed Ivy in a storm. Was that to cover their tracks or to make sure she wouldn't be discovered soon or that no one would come to the inn and catch them in the act? That would mean it was premeditated.

"Lucky thing we still have plenty of suspects, and I know how we can catch the killer," Agnes announced, her eyes twinkling with mischief.

"How?" Betty asked, looking skeptical.

"We stage a little clue fake." Agnes grinned, clearly pleased with herself.

"What in the world is a clue fake?" Doris asked, scratching her head.

While the rest of us exchanged confused glances. Agnes waved her bran-muffin top in the air like a magician with a wand. "I saw it on one of my shows. We tell the suspects something about the crime that isn't true, and the one who corrects us is the killer!"

"Would they be that dumb?" I asked.

"You'd be surprised," Doris said, breaking off a piece of her scone and bending down to give it to Prancer. The tiny Chihuahua hoovered it up, wagging his tail with glee. If these ladies kept coming over, Prancer was going to need a diet plan.

"Did you invite them all?" Betty inquired, bringing me back to the task at hand.

I sifted through the invitations, tossing them in a pile. "Miranda, Cecelia, Eliot, Simon... I guess Benjamin is out, but I invited him. Oh, and George."

Agnes's muffin-wielding hand paused in midair. "This is going to be interesting," she declared, and I couldn't help but agree. The clue-fake idea was outlandish, but then again, so was everything else about this case.

"It can't be George!" Betty gasped.

"Why not?" I asked, sipping my tea.

"He's so nice, dear. Nicer than my late Harold, and I married him!" she added, winking at Agnes.

"It's usually the nice ones," Agnes chimed in, her voice dripping with the wisdom of a thousand TV detective shows. "Like that charming man on *Murder Street* last week. Lovely smile, terrible with an axe."

Doris nodded her agreement, brushing crumbs from her knitting project. "And let's not forget George's motive—a classic murder of passion. Ivy just didn't return his feelings, poor thing."

I pressed my lips together. I thought George was nice, too, but I really didn't know him well.

"My money is on Miranda." Betty's lips puckered as if she'd just bitten into a lemon. "She's in love with George. That's a pretty strong motive to do away with the competition, don't you think?"

"What about Simon?" I asked, nibbling on a gingerbread cookie. "Nick said he was blackmailing people. Maybe Ivy found out and threatened to expose him. That would be a strong motive to kill her."

"You've been seeing Nick?" Agnes's eyes sparkled, and I could almost see the gears turning in her head.

I frowned. "No, but I was at his bakery to pick up pastries for the book club meeting, and I ran into him at the tree lot."

"Oh sure. Right," Agnes said, looking smug.

"Do you think Simon will come to the party? He doesn't have much Christmas party spirit," Doris said.

"He will for free food." Betty emphasized the word *free.*

"Speaking of food, what are you having?" Agnes inquired, her eyes gleaming with culinary curiosity.

"Oh, the usual Christmas fare. Roast turkey, glazed ham, mashed potatoes with gravy, cranberry sauce, and an array of pies and desserts. I'm having some catered and, of course, some of my own creations."

"Sounds delicious," Betty said.

"If you want, we can come over that day and help you set up," Agnes said. "And if you're having Nick cater something…"

"Yes, I am, as a matter of fact. I can't bake nearly as good as he does."

"Perfect." Agnes sat back in her seat. "Then we'll make sure not to forget to put up the mistletoe."

CHAPTER 22

The next few days were a whirlwind of booking last-minute caterers, making a menu of foods I could prepare, and acquiring the dinnerware, tables, and decor for the party.

Agnes, Doris, and Betty had shown up just as promised, wearing festive Christmas sweaters. Doris had drafted Maggie to help with the setup.

"Do you have those antlers still?" Betty asked, scooping Prancer up into her arms. Her eyes sparkled with mischief.

Prancer shot me a look, his tiny eyes narrowing. I could have sworn he understood English when it suited him.

I chuckled. "Betty, if you dress him as a reindeer, I can't promise he won't plot your downfall."

Agnes waved a hand dismissively, her arms full of glittering decorations. "Oh, Prancer will look adorable, won't you, sweetheart?" she cooed.

Prancer's response was a dubious tilt of the head.

The women and I—and a highly skeptical Prancer—scrambled around, setting tables, fluffing pillows, and arranging treats. The aromas of baking spices mingled with the tangy pine of the Christmas tree.

I'd hired servers to circle with trays of gourmet hors d'oeuvres and keep the chafing dishes brimming with warm food during the party. In the bustling kitchen, I found myself juggling a culinary circus—everything from succulent roasts to homemade dinner rolls. A twirl here, a whisk there, and a quick dash to make sure the flambé wasn't living up to its name too literally.

I handed Betty a tray of Aunt Ivy's famous cranberry-glazed puff pastries. "Here, put these on that table—no, not that one. The one with the red cloth. Oh, heavens, not near the candles!"

Betty's eyes widened, and she darted the pastries away from the open flame like they were about to explode. Disaster averted—or more accurately, pastries preserved.

Agnes was stringing lights, her Christmas sweater

glowing with such intensity I half expected reindeer to land on the roof. "Annie, where's the extension cord?"

"In the left drawer of the server. Under the occupancy permit that Simon insisted must be displayed for everyone to see."

Agnes rolled her eyes. "I do hope he shows up."

While Doris wrestled with a tangled string of garland, Prancer leaped and barked at the shiny nemesis. His little tail wagged with enthusiasm, each bark a declaration of war against the glittering foe.

"Have you thought up the fake out for our killer?" Betty asked, her voice lowering to an almost conspiratorial whisper.

A smile played at the corner of my mouth as I nodded. "Yes, I'm going to say a priceless antique clock that has been handed down through our family was missing, and we think someone broke in to steal it. Ivy caught them, and they killed her. The mantel is beside the stairs, and I've already made an empty spot." I pointed, adding a touch of theatrics.

Maggie's face crinkled into a frown, her concern apparent. "But what if that's too dangerous? What if the killer feels trapped and lashes out?"

I paused, the last tray in my hand, feeling the weight of her words. Her worry was contagious, but Agnes was quick to cut through it, her voice brimming with common sense. "Honey, there's not much a desperate killer can do in a room full of people, especially with all of us watching."

I placed the last tray on the table, my fingers lingering on the cool porcelain. We all stood back to survey our handiwork, and I was struck by the transformation of the room.

Fairy lights, elegantly strung along the walls, cast a warm, inviting glow. They mingled with the rich, festive hues of red and green from the garlands, wreaths, and baubles that adorned every available surface. The majestic Christmas tree stood in the corner, the ornaments that Nick and I had put on it glistening.

The scent of cinnamon, cloves, and roasted nuts filled the air, mingling with the heady fragrance of pine from the fresh greenery. Soft Christmas music played in the background. I'd chosen jazzy renditions of Christmas carols mixed in with a few old favorites.

"It's perfect," I whispered, feeling a rare moment of satisfaction and triumph. But underneath the pride, a thread of tension pulled tight. The room was dressed for celebration, but it was also a stage for a dangerous game. The thought hung in the air, a subtle chill that not even the crackling fireplace could quite banish.

The others must have felt it, too, their eyes meeting mine with a mixture of excitement and uncertainty.

Doris clapped her hands and looked at her watch. "We'd better get going. Only two hours to party time, and I need to change into my party dress!" she exclaimed.

The others quickly nodded in a flurry of agreement with the sudden realization that we were indeed on a tight schedule.

"I haven't even picked out my shoes yet!" Agnes cried, grabbing her coat.

"Shoes? I need to decide on the earrings," Maggie added, her voice tinged with mock horror as she pulled on her scarf.

I found myself laughing, the tension easing as we all scurried around, getting ready to depart. Prancer yapped excitedly, sensing the change in energy, his tail wagging like a metronome set to a lively tempo.

As they were all heading out the door, Betty turned back, a playful glint in her eye. "What does one wear to catch a killer?" she asked, her voice dripping with curiosity and mischief.

I leaned against the doorframe, a smile playing on my lips. "Something stunning yet sensible. And don't forget the most important accessory," I added, tapping my temple. "A sharp mind."

Betty chuckled, her laughter ringing through the crisp winter air as she closed the door behind her.

I was left standing in the festive room, surrounded by the anticipation of joy and the shadow of danger. The clock was ticking, both for the party and for our plan to catch the killer. I glanced at the empty spot on the mantel one more time, feeling a shiver that had nothing to do with the cold.

With a determined sigh, I headed upstairs to change. It was time to dress for the occasion, after all. The menu was set, the decor in place, and the trap laid.

"Don't worry, it's only for one night," I said to Prancer as he tried to wriggle out of my grasp. The antlers I'd found in the kitchen wobbled on his head, but they did look adorable with his red Nordic-snowflake-design sweater. A whimper, a twist, and a certain look in those big brown eyes—Prancer's silent plea to let him be—gave me a pang of guilt. But oh, the cuteness was worth it.

I'd changed into a sky-blue satin sheath dress that complemented my eyes. My dark hair was down instead of in the ponytail I usually wore. A flutter of excitement, mixed with nervous anticipation, danced in my stomach as I glanced around the room. Was it too late to reconsider playing hostess? The doorbell rang, saving me from my thoughts.

Caterers. Right on time.

I let them in, and they got set up in the kitchen. The servers were right behind them.

"Can you circulate the trays through these rooms?" I gestured, showing them around the rooms and the kitchen and explaining the flow of the evening. Their nods and smiles were reassuring. With thirty minutes to go, my hands were shaking like I'd downed four cups of espresso.

I hadn't realized how important it was to me for everything to go right so I could make a good impression and assure everyone I would fit in as seamlessly as Ivy had.

Nick's arrival was a welcome distraction, his eyes widening as he took in my outfit. "Well, someone scrubs up nice."

I laughed, my cheeks burning. I eyed the tower of bakery boxes he carried. "Wow, that looks like a lot." Peeking behind the boxes, I saw that Nick was dressed up too. He looked good, but I refrained from saying so.

"Just what you ordered." He winked. "Okay, maybe a few extra."

I showed him to the kitchen and got him set up with some tiered trays he could use for the pastries then checked back in on the caterers. Everything was ready. Now all we needed were the guests.

The doorbell rang again, snapping me back to reality. Time to put on my party-hostess hat. I smoothed my skirt and opened the door.

First through the door was Maggie. Her black velvet dress shimmered like the night sky, adorned only with delicate diamond ear studs and a matching halo pendant. She introduced the handsome man with her as her husband, Danny. He was charming and offered a warm smile as he shook my hand.

"Glad Maggie has a partner in crime that's her age," he joked, his eyes twinkling with amusement. "Someone to keep her out of mischief. She hangs around with Doris too much and gets into trouble."

Maggie and I exchanged knowing smiles, her eyes promising future escapades. "Oh, we'll be friends, all right. But keeping out of mischief? No guarantees there."

Then came Agnes, Doris, and Betty, each donning her own unique style of clothing. Agnes wore a flamboyant red dress that matched her lipstick, accentuated with a dramatic feather boa that seemed to have a personality of its own. Doris was in silver, with pearls at her neck, exuding a timeless elegance. Betty, on the other hand, was sporting a crocheted bolero jacket that had the audacity to be both vintage and trendy, paired with a playful floral dress that swished as she moved.

"Betty, that jacket is fabulous," I said.

Betty twirled, showing off her outfit. "Why, thank you, dear. I made it myself."

Prancer, adorned in his red Nordic-snowflake-design sweater, yipped around them, practically begging for compliments. The ladies obliged, cooing over how adorable he looked with the antlers on.

"Gram! It's great to see you." Nick appeared at my side.

Agnes leaned in to plant a smooch on Nick's cheek, leaving a triumphant trail of red lipstick. "A little something to match my ensemble." She winked, her laughter echoing her lively attire.

As more townspeople arrived, the room filled with chatter. Compliments on my new venture were generously sprinkled through conversations. The warm glow of the chandeliers reflected off polished wood and fine china, the soft strains of Christmas music adding to the festive ambiance.

Everyone seemed genuinely pleased with the inn's opening, their warm smiles and enthusiastic congratulations washing over me like a comforting embrace.

Geraldine, from the town hall, greeted me with a

knowing smile. "Such a lovely party, and the place looks great." She gestured to the room with her cocktail.

"Thank you very much."

"So glad you're taking up Ivy's charitable spirit," she chirped.

A pang of guilt hit me about the ledger I'd never found, but I managed a gracious smile in return.

The Snowman Sculpture Showdown next week loomed over me like a dark cloud, and thoughts of picking up the trash weren't exactly thrilling. "I'm happy to do anything I can do to help."

My eyes wandered across the room and landed on Cecelia. She was draped in a fluffy hot-pink outfit trimmed with the puffiest fur at the sleeves and hem. It screamed designer chic, or perhaps it just screamed. She sure did go in for flair.

Next to her stood a stunning figure in a tight gold lamé dress. She looked kind of familiar, but I didn't know very many people in town. She glanced my way, catching my eye, and it hit me. Chief Barnes. Who knew she was such a stunner under that police uniform? No wonder Nick had fallen for her.

Was that a glint of suspicion in her eye? I looked away as fast as I could.

As I moved through the crowd, exchanging pleasantries and accepting pats on the back, I could feel a sense of belonging settle within me. The town, with its quaint charm and close-knit community, had accepted me, and the excitement of starting this new adventure was blossoming in my heart.

Gone were the lingering thoughts of my old job, the rigid schedules, and the endless demands. The idea of a fresh start took away the sting of the way things had ended at the last job. Hopefully, things wouldn't go south here when we tried to trick the killer into confessing.

I was starting to wonder if that was such a good idea. I was nursing a rum punch along with my second thoughts about Agnes's scheme when I spotted the three ladies in the corner, motioning to me.

"Our suspects are all here," Doris announced, scanning the room with the practiced eye of a seasoned detective-show binger.

"Poor George looks like he's auditioning for a tragedy," I mused, recalling the lone tear I'd spotted in his eye when I'd greeted him earlier.

Behind him, Cecelia darted away from Prancer, who was parading about the room, accepting treats like royalty accepting tribute. Cecelia's expression was a priceless blend of disdain and fear.

I wondered if I should put him upstairs. Some

people might not love dogs, and I didn't want to suffer the gastronomic consequences of what people were feeding him. Besides, Simon might try to use having an animal in the inn against me.

Next to Cecelia was Miranda. She was bedecked with so much jewelry she looked ready to tip over. Every step she took, following George, sent chandeliers of diamonds and emeralds swinging like tiny, sparkly wrecking balls.

"One gust of wind and she's a human wind chime," Agnes said, pointing at her.

"I think George is actually running away from her." Doris added.

"Check out Simon." Betty pointed to the end of the table, where Simon stood alone, scarfing down food as though it might flee from his plate. As near as I could tell, the entire party had been avoiding him.

Agnes put her plate down on the table, brushed her hands together, and gave us a serious look. "Ladies, it's showtime."

CHAPTER 24

Agnes, Betty, and Doris took off in opposite directions. Agnes made a beeline for Cecelia, who was hovering around the punch bowl. Agnes must have said something funny because the two of them started laughing, then Agnes hooked her arm through Cecelia's and led her toward the fireplace.

Betty latched on to George. She reeled him in with a knowing smile, leaving Miranda to trail behind them, casting jealous glares at Betty.

Poor Doris, though. She must have pulled the short straw. She sidled up to Simon at the food table. Whatever she said had his eyes flicking over to the fire. He nodded, and they proceeded to join the rest of us, Simon looking about as thrilled as a cat offered a bath.

Maggie must have been in on it, too, because she walked up to the group with Eliot.

Prancer, not to be left out, trotted over and stood beside me.

Once the suspects were corralled, milling about with forced smiles and thinly veiled curiosity, Agnes blurted, "Will the police reopen your aunt's case, given your new suspicions, Annie?"

Everyone turned to me, faces frowning. I could feel the collective gaze pinning me to the spot. Even Prancer looked up at me before turning his attention to the suspects. He sniffed at them one by one.

Finally, Simon broke the silence, his voice dripping with faux innocence. "What suspicions are those?"

"I, er..." I stammered, suddenly feeling a bout of nerves. Maybe this wasn't such a good idea. But Agnes, Doris, and Betty were staring at me expectantly. Leaning in and lowering my voice, I said, "I don't think Aunt Ivy was alone that night. I think there might have been a theft. She had a priceless antique clock on the mantel, and now it's gone..."

Everyone's eyes swiveled to the mantel.

Cecelia gasped, her hand flying to her chest.

Miranda, mid cream-puff bite, froze like a statue.

Simon's eyes lit up with a mysterious glint that begged the question, "What was it worth?"

Eliot just stared at me, a slight frown on his face.

Prancer skittered about, eyeing Cecelia's shiny hem. It probably reminded him of the tree garland. I shot him a warning glance. *I really should have put him upstairs.*

George narrowed his eyes at me. "You must be mistaken. I don't think Ivy had a clock there."

"Aha!" Agnes pointed at George. "You're the—"

But before she could finish, I jabbed her in the ribs. Something wasn't right. Eliot had left footprints in the snow that night, so it had been snowing, with low visibility.

Agnes removed my elbow from her ribs and continued, still pointing at George. "The killer!"

George's eyes widened, and his face turned red. "What are you talking about? Ivy fell."

Prancer chose that moment to use Cecelia's hem as a play toy, tugging at it and almost ripping it from her dress. Cecelia jumped back. "Get away from me, you little monster. I'm not going to let you gore me again!"

Again?

And then it all clicked into place.

Cecelia had said she'd seen George leaving the inn when she was on her way to the observatory, but why would she go there during a snowstorm? The skies had been clouded, with nothing to observe. Had she lied to frame George?

The garland around Prancer's fake antlers, when I found him, had been purple. I glanced at the tree. Aunt Ivy only had red, green, silver, and gold, but Cecelia's dresses were always in pink and purple and had the garland-like trim.

Ivy had worked with Cecelia on the charities.

The charity fund was losing money.

Cecelia loved the finer things in life, but rumor had it her finances were in decline.

Ivy had done the bookkeeping, but the Elf Extravaganza ledger was nowhere to be found.

Was that because Ivy had discovered Cecelia was embezzling from the charity?

Had she confronted Cecelia? Had Cecelia tried to pay her off and Ivy ripped up the check in the kitchen, then Cecelia pushed her down the stairs and took the ledger?

"It's not George," I declared, a sudden clarity hitting me. "It's Cecelia!"

Cecelia's face twisted, her eyes narrowing. "Excuse me?"

"You embezzled from the charity fund, and Aunt Ivy caught you," I said, my voice firm but my hands shaking slightly. A thrill of suspense tingled up my spine as I laid out the pieces of the puzzle.

"No, you have no proof," Cecelia stammered, her posture defiant.

I felt a smirk tugging at the corner of my mouth. "You wrote the threatening notes, and I'm sure I can prove that. I have some contacts that specialize in handwriting analysis, you know. And about those pieces of ripped-up check I found in the kitchen? You probably thought you'd picked it all up." My heart pounded in my chest as I watched realization dawn in her eyes.

Cecelia's face went pale, and she started to back away. "Well, I... I don't have to stand here and listen to this nonsense."

I took a step toward her, determination fueling me. "Oh, I think you do."

With a cry, Cecelia turned and bolted, her heels clattering on the floor.

"Grab her!" Agnes shouted.

"Right behind you!" Betty yelled.

"Look out!" Doris shouted as we all ran at the same time, tripping over each other and letting Cecelia get a head start.

Thankfully, Chief Barnes had noticed what was going on. She sprinted to the door, blocking Cecelia's escape, and tackled her in a move that would make a linebacker envious. Handcuffs appeared from some-where—seriously, where had she hidden those in that tight dress?

"Cecelia Rothschild, you're under arrest!" Barnes proclaimed, her face flushed with triumph.

THE PARTY BROKE up shortly after the arrest, and Agnes, Betty, Doris, and Nick stayed to help me clean up.

"I can't believe it was Cecelia all along," Betty exclaimed, shaking her head as she scrubbed a stub-born stain. "To think she was stealing from charity!"

Agnes, ever the practical one, was focused on wrapping leftover pastries. "Well, she's caught now. That's all that matters."

Nick was fiddling with a tray of cream puffs, but I could tell his mind was elsewhere.

There was a knock on the door, and Agnes rushed to open it. Chief Barnes herself strode in, her expres-sion serious.

"Evening, all," she said, nodding to the room, her gaze lingering on me just a fraction too long.

"Chief." I nodded a greeting, feeling an uneasy

twinge. Why was she back here? And why did I detect a hint of tension between her and Nick? Had old feelings been stirred? "What brings you here?"

She leaned against the counter, every inch the small-town sheriff with a secret or two still up her sleeve. "I wanted to bring you up to speed on the case. I never truly closed the case as an accident. I just made it appear that way."

My eyes widened, and I exchanged a wary glance with Nick.

"I had a hunch that the suspects—yourself included…" Barnes's eyes narrowed as she eyed me as if maybe I had actually been her *prime* suspect. "Someone would make a mistake if they thought they'd gotten away with it."

"So you were playing us all along," Doris said, her voice filled with awe.

"In a manner of speaking," Barnes replied, her smile not quite reaching her eyes.

I tried to laugh, but the sound was more of a nervous chuckle. "You certainly fooled us."

"Yes, well, I was narrowing in on Cecelia and gathering evidence. That's what we do in *real* police work." She shot a glance at Agnes. "I knew it was her but needed to get all my ducks in a row before I could arrest her."

"Looks like we did you a favor, then," Betty said.

"I don't know about that. But she's in jail now," Barnes said. "She's already confessed. Said your aunt crossed the line when she told her to put the money back or she'd tell on her. She tried to pay her off, but Ivy would have none of it."

Crossed the line. That was in the note. And the check pieces must have been from Cecelia trying to pay Ivy off.

Barnes continued. "And she didn't like you looking into things. Said she left you a note? You must have forgotten to tell me about that."

I blushed. She must have been referring to the note I'd found in the door.

Barnes nodded as if she could read my mind. "Anyway, we found the Elf Extravaganza ledger in Cecelia's house. And a dress with some sparkly purple trim missing."

"That was what was on Prancer's antlers when I found him," I said.

Barnes nodded, her eyes never leaving mine. "Indeed."

After a bit more strained chatting, Chief Barnes left, leaving us to our cleaning and thoughts.

In the kitchen, Nick and I found ourselves alone,

snacking on some of the pastries that still needed to be put away.

Prancer danced around at our feet.

"I guess I should give him a treat. After all, he did provide the big clue that solved the case." I broke off a small piece of cream puff and fed it to him.

"You know," Nick said, looking at me with a playful glint in his eye, "we eat a lot of pastries together. Maybe sometime we could get together for a real meal."

I felt a flush rise to my cheeks, but I met his gaze squarely. "I think I'd like that. And we have something to celebrate."

"We do? You mean finding the killer?"

"That, and I just booked my first guest for the inn." I held up my phone, which displayed the booking app. The reservation had come in while all the hoopla with Cecelia was happening, and I'd just noticed it.

Just then, Agnes stumbled into the room, nearly tripping over her own feet.

"Gram!" Nick raised a brow at his grandmother. "Were you spying on us?"

Agnes looked flustered, her cheeks a delightful shade of crimson. "Spying? No! I was just..." She looked up at the top of the doorway. "Cleaning this sprig of mistletoe."

We all burst into laughter, the sound echoing through the inn as the tension of the past few weeks lifted. Dinner with Nick, justice served, and friends to share it all with—life in Yule Notch was looking pretty sweet.

Cozy Mysteries

Juniper Holiday Cozy Mysteries

***

Halloween Party Murder
Thanksgiving Dinner Death
Who Slayed The Santas?
Masquerade Party Murder
My Fatal Valentine

Mystic Notch
Cat Cozy Mystery Series

* * *

Ghostly Paws

A Spirited Tail
A Mew To A Kill
Paws and Effect
Probable Paws
A Whisker of a Doubt
Wrong Side of the Claw
Claw and Order

**Oyster Cove Guesthouse
Cat Cozy Mystery Series**

***

A Twist in the Tail
A Whisker in the Dark
A Purrfect Alibi

Moorecliff Manor Cat Cozy Mystery Series

* * *

Dead in the Dining Room
Stabbed in the Solarium
Homicide in the Hydrangeas
Lifeless in the Library

Silver Hollow

Paranormal Cozy Mystery Series

***

A Spell of Trouble (Book 1)

Spell Disaster (Book 2)

Nothing to Croak About (Book 3)

Cry Wolf (Book 4)

Shear Magic (Book 5)

Blackmoore Sisters

Cozy Mystery Series

* * *

Dead Wrong

Dead & Buried

Dead Tide

Buried Secrets

Deadly Intentions

A Grave Mistake

Spell Found

Fatal Fortune

Hidden Secrets

Kate Diamond Mystery Adventures

***

Hidden Agemda (Book 1)
Ancient Hiss Story (Book 2)
Heist Society (Book 3)

Mooseamuck Island
Cozy Mystery Series
* * *

A Zen For Murder
A Crabby Killer
A Treacherous Treasure

Lexy Baker
Cozy Mystery Series
* * *

Lexy Baker Cozy Mystery Series Boxed Set Vol 1 (Books 1-4)

Or buy the books separately:

Killer Cupcakes
Dying For Danish
Murder, Money and Marzipan
3 Bodies and a Biscotti

Brownies, Bodies & Bad Guys
Bake, Battle & Roll
Wedded Blintz
Scones, Skulls & Scams
Ice Cream Murder
Mummified Meringues
Brutal Brulee (Novella)
No Scone Unturned
Cream Puff Killer
Never Say Pie

Lady Katherine Regency Mysteries

***

An Invitation to Murder (Book 1)
The Baffling Burglaries of Bath (Book 2)
Murder at the Ice Ball (Book 3)
A Murderous Affair (Book 4)
Murder on Charles Street (Book 5)

Hazel Martin Historical Mystery Series

***

Murder at Lowry House (book 1)
Murder by Misunderstanding (book 2)

Sam Mason Mysteries
(As L. A. Dobbs)

***

Telling Lies (Book 1)

Keeping Secrets (Book 2)

Exposing Truths (Book 3)

Betraying Trust (Book 4)

Killing Dreams (Book 5)

Romantic Comedy

***

Corporate Chaos Series

In Over Her Head (book 1)

Can't Stand the Heat (book 2)

What Goes Around Comes Around (book 3)

Careful What You Wish For (4)

Contemporary Romance

***

Reluctant Romance

Sweet Romance (Written As Annie Dobbs)
Firefly Inn Series

***

Another Chance (Book 1)

Another Wish (Book 2)

Hometown Hearts Series

***

No Getting Over You (Book 1)

A Change of Heart (Book 2)

Sweet Mountain Billionaires

***

Jaded Billionaire (Book 1)

A Billion Reasons Not To Fall In Love (Book 2)

——

Regency Romance

* * *

Scandals and Spies Series:
Kissing The Enemy

ABOUT THE AUTHOR

USA Today best-selling Author, Leighann Dobbs, has had a passion for reading since she was old enough to hold a book, but she didn't put pen to paper until much later in life. After a twenty-year career as a software engineer, with a few side trips into selling antiques and making jewelry, she realized you can't make a living reading books, so she tried her hand at writing them and discovered she had a passion for that, too! She lives in New Hampshire with her husband, Bruce, their trusty Chihuahua mix, Mojo, and beautiful rescue cat, Kitty.

Find out about her latest books by signing up at:
    https://leighanndobbscozymysteries.gr8.com

Connect with Leighann on Facebook:
    https://www.facebook.com/groups/
718049055015420

www.ingramcontent.com/pod-product-compliance
Lightning Source LLC
Chambersburg PA
CBHW061308210726
48293CB00003B/1162